A VIC TYLER NOVEL

CHANGE OF LOCATION

GB COPELAND

ISBN 979-8-9913299-2-7 (Paperback)

ISBN 979-8-9913299-3-4 (eBook)

Book Cover Design and Interior Formatting by 100Covers.

Dedicated to all who have worn the uniform.

Now that he'd felt the fire, he didn't want to go back to the ashes.

CHAPTER 1

Jake Connor, widowed way too young, knew what it was like to make himself a sandwich with tears splashing down on his hands. Several years prior, the former police officer had lost his wife and two-year-old son to a drunk driver. That tragedy was followed by the death of both his parents, barely a year after he'd lost his wife and son. Unconsolable and lost, Jake had retired from his police career after just twelve years on the job and, now forty years old, he was mostly alone in the world.

An only child, he inherited a substantial amount of money as well as a house on Spirit Lake in northern Idaho from his parents. Once he retired from the Yakima, Washington Police Department Jake had moved to the house on Spirit Lake, thinking his good memories of the place would assuage his grief and help him feel better. It hadn't worked. The good memories, as well as the influx of happy people in the summer, only served to accentuate his present loneliness and he sold the place after just a few months. He found a house with a detached shop which sat on a few acres near Boekel Road, a little east of the small town of Rathdrum, Idaho. The place suited him: It was in the part of the state he considered home, there were few other houses nearby, and he was left alone to do as he pleased.

For the most part, Jake's only companion was his dead wife's cat, Luna. The solid gray cat had stuck it out with him through everything, and he made sure she had a good life. When he first moved to the house on Boekel Road she had really wanted to go outside, but he never let her because he heard and saw coyotes all the time. Now, years later, she was a little older and more content staying inside.

Jake, over time, developed a habit of having imaginary conversations with his wife and son. He knew the conversations weren't real, but he usually didn't have anyone else to talk to and they seemed to help him cope. At the end of the day, he would tell his wife what he'd been doing, and he would tell his son how much he loved him and how proud of him he was. Sometimes he would get his guitar and sing a song or two for them. For the past couple of years, he believed his wife had been sending him a message during the conversations, a simple message that he should remember her and his son, but that he should start living his life again. Logically, he knew the message was what he needed to hear. Emotionally though, he was far less certain. He felt she had been the love of his life, and without her, there was no one else for him. He'd been on no dates since her death and made no efforts at all to meet other women. He couldn't gin up any interest in travelling or in having new experiences. Still, her message for him to live his life persisted and, occasionally, he allowed himself to think about what that might mean.

Phone calls and visits from his former coworkers had dwindled over the years but there were two other retired officers he kept in close contact with—Doc and Vic Tyler. Doc, a physician, had been a reserve police officer and had retired with his lovely wife to nearby Coeur d'Alene. Vic had also retired and had moved to Las Vegas. Jake knew Vic had been going through some tough times down in the Southwest, but hoped his difficulties were over. Twice in the past few months he and Doc had been on the verge of going to Las Vegas to help him out, but his situation seemed to have stabilized for the time being.

The three had been on Yakima's SWAT team together for many years. Doc held black belts in several martial arts and, while in Yakima, they had frequently trained in his basement where he had a large room set up with wrestling mats.

Jake spent a lot of time in the shop on his property building furniture. Besides hiking and working out at the excellent gym in Rathdrum, it was his main hobby. Currently he was working on a black walnut hall table with tapered legs—he'd cut the tapers on his table saw with a tapering jig and was now smoothing away the blade marks with a hand plane. The early January temperature was only about ten degrees, but a propane furnace kept his shop nice and warm. He was almost finished for the day when he saw he had a call from Vic, and he picked up the phone. "Hey Vic, what's going on?"

"A bit of an emergency I'm afraid, Jake. Are you at your place and near a computer?"

"I'm in the shop, give me just a minute." He shut everything down in the shop and made the short walk to his house, where he turned on his desktop computer and turned again to the phone. "I'm here Vic."

"OK. Well, you know about all the drama Nina and I have had with the cartels down here. There's a woman that Nina and I are very close to. She started as an informant but is now more like a sister to us—it's a long story that I'll save for later. I'll just tell you she saved our lives, and we'd do most anything for her. Anyway, she's a witness in the upcoming court matters and she's been travelling around the western U.S., trying to keep away from the cartel. She has a Garmin GPS device with her, and Nina can always see her location and movement because she has access to the device's tracking. A few hours ago she was in her 4Runner up by Mirror Lake, not that far from you. The track shows that she stopped suddenly, then headed off at a running pace through the woods, headed roughly to the south. After a mile or so the track slowed down to a walk, then a very slow walk, and now it's been stuck in one place for ten minutes."

"Damn, that doesn't sound good. FYI, it's ten degrees here right now and it's three o'clock in the afternoon. Once the sun goes down in an hour or so it'll be close to zero. How far did she make it after leaving her car?"

"About ten miles. She's in excellent shape, and about thirty-five years old. But we have no idea how she's dressed, and this looks like hypothermia to us. She's not answering her phone. And there's another problem, Jake. We don't want to create any official records involving her, which is another thing I'll explain later. Also, this is a tough woman, don't count her out."

"Understood. But the woods are thick and hilly up there man, ten miles is a long way in them in the winter with the snow. It's not flat like where I live here on the Rathdrum prairie. She could easily have broken a sweat early on and now the dampness could be making her even colder. Do you have her current coordinates?"

Jake entered the latitude and longitude provided by Vic into a maps program. He saw that the location was a little east and north of the town of Bayview, about a half-hour from his house. She wasn't too far from Cape Horn Road and there was an unpaved road which, if drivable, led from Cape Horn Road to an area within about three hundred yards of her. He memorized the curves of the road and the terrain features so that he'd know where to park his truck.

"OK, I've got her location and should be able to get to her within about forty-five minutes." He explained the road situation to Vic. "If I'm reading the terrain correctly, she's uphill from where I'm going to park, so I'll get her in my truck one way or the other. I'm going to get moving right now. Can you call Doc and give him the information, maybe he can respond as well? She may well need him, and it's a good idea to have a backup."

"Will do. And Jake? Watch yourself, we have no idea what's going on with her."

"Always do."

Jake quickly removed his trail runners and pulled on a pair of insulated winter boots. He grabbed a heavy jacket, hat, and gloves, as well as his daypack which he kept stocked for emergencies. Within a couple minutes he was in his black Tundra pickup and moving towards Bayview. It was his habit to always keep his truck full of fuel. He wanted to get to the woman's location while there was still a little daylight left and so drove as quickly as he could. After a few minutes Doc called to let him know he was on the way and would contact him once he arrived where Jake was going to park.

Once on Cape Horn Road, he found the unpaved road—it was not plowed but the snow was packed down well enough so he could drive on it. Moving to his parking spot, he shut his truck off, put on his heavy clothing items, and headed uphill. After about two hundred yards he reached a clearing where the terrain leveled off and began looking for the woman at the tree line on the far side of the area of open ground. He didn't see her at first, but as he got closer he saw a bit of red color under a downed tree. When he reached the spot, he saw that she had wedged herself under the downed tree and was inside a lightweight "bivvy", a sack normally used as a cover for a sleeping bag. However, she had no sleeping bag and was simply curled up in the bivvy with only a light jacket and hat on. It was not nearly enough insulation for the snow and frigid temperatures. She was using a daypack as a pillow. He removed one of his gloves and checked her pulse—she had a slow pulse and was breathing, but slowly. Her face and lips had a blue tinge, and she looked like a dead person to him. He thought about how to get her to the truck and decided it would be easiest and quickest if he just left her in the bivvy and slid her down the hill. Grabbing her pack with one hand and the top of her bivvy with the other, he began the downhill walk back to his truck, which was not difficult and he could move quickly. He remembered that unconscious, hypothermic people should not be jostled too much and tried to avoid as many bumps as he could. As he reached his truck, he saw Doc pulling up behind him in his vintage maroon Mercedes G-wagon. Doc walked up and took over immediately.

"All right. Start your truck and crank that heat, and I mean crank it all the way. We're going to put her in the backseat of your truck, get her out of this bivvy, then get her out of this coat and hat so the heat can reach her." They quickly got that done, and Doc also removed her frozen shoes and wet socks. He then climbed in the back with her, closed the door, and instructed Jake to get in the driver's seat and to keep his door shut. Doc took her pulse and monitored her breathing for a minute.

"Well, she's in the danger zone but otherwise looks healthy and uninjured. If we can warm her up quickly she has a chance." Doc pointed to a shoulder holster that the woman was wearing and removed a pistol from it. He handed the pistol to Jake. "We don't want her to come to and start shooting at us. Only one emergency at a time. I'll follow you to your place, and I'll be able to check her over a little more completely there."

They got their vehicles turned around and began the drive back. After about ten minutes, the woman began to stir and moan a little, which Jake hoped was a good sign. He made a quick call to Vic, gave him an update, and told him he'd have more information for him soon. Once at his house, Jake had Doc open the door while he carried the woman inside. He laid her on a couch, which they slid close to the freestanding wood stove in the living room. Jake started a fire while Doc checked the woman's pulse, breathing, blood pressure, temperature, and blood oxygen level. The woman continued to move a little and to moan, with her lips moving slightly. Jake thought her face looked a little less blue.

"I think she's coming around," said Doc. "She needs the basics, which are shelter, hydration, and food. She has shelter now, so let's work on hydration. She needs something warm and caffeine-free to drink. Do you have any chicken broth, or something like that?"

Jake had some bouillon cubes, and he heated some water and a cube up in the microwave while Doc tried to talk to the woman and to wake her up. After a minute she opened her eyes and then suddenly sat up, looking wildly around her. Doc spoke to her in a calm voice, telling her that he and Jake were friends of Vic and Nina, that she was safe, that they were going to give her some food and something warm to drink, and that she could call Nina on the phone in just a few minutes. She patted herself down, as if checking to make sure she hadn't been disrobed or molested, then looked at Doc and Jake closely, one at a time. Finally, she spoke.

"You guys look like cops. Did you work with Vic or Nina, and if so, where? And, by the way, where is my weapon?"

They told her they'd both worked with Vic in Yakima for many years, that her pistol was out in the truck, and that they'd return it to her shortly. It seemed to make her feel better. Jake gave her a cup of hot broth, which she took and began to sip. It occurred to Jake that during the entire episode he hadn't heard her name, and he asked her for it.

"My name," she said, "is Xana. It's spelled with an X, but pronounced with a Z."

CHAPTER 2

After Xana had some broth and a light meal, Jake called Vic and Nina and put them on speakerphone so everyone could discuss what had happened to Xana. After the greetings, Xana began to tell her story.

"Well, I think this really is a case of me being a little too bored and a little too curious. So, the whole time I was involved with the cartel, I'd occasionally hear about a business called Preston Security, which is across the state line in Spokane Valley. They're what I would call mid-level meth and fentanyl dealers, though I don't remember hearing about them being into prostitution or human trafficking. Anyway, lately I've just been doing my usual thing, going from town to town, seeing what there is to see. I visited Walla Walla, the Tri-Cities, Yakima, and then made my way to Spokane. And I don't know, maybe it's because of the dreary winter days or something—but I was bored and had an urge to swing by the Preston Security office, just to see what it looked like and how big an operation it was. I found a place to park where I could watch for a while. After about an hour, a white pickup truck that had the Preston Security logo on the side drove out of the office area and the driver was really eyeballing me—he lifted his phone and snapped a photo of me as he went by.

"I knew that was my cue to leave. But I hadn't even made it a block before two more trucks pulled out of the office area and started following me. All three of them were right on my ass. My first thought was to go across the state line into Idaho, thinking maybe that would stop them, but it didn't, and they just kept right on me. I should have called the police, but I was getting stubborn and thought I could lose them…but I wasn't sure where I was. I remember I was headed towards Sandpoint on Highway 95, and I did a quick and illegal U-turn. They did the same thing and stayed with me. Somehow, I ended up by Mirror Lake on Talache Road in the middle of nowhere. That's where they made their move. Two of them pulled up on my driver's side and forced me into a snowbank and, because of what I know of them, I figured they would kill me if they got their hands on me. I grabbed my keys and my daypack, which had my Garmin hooked to it, squeezed out the passenger door, and made a run into the woods. The snow there had a bit of crust on top, so I could sort of dance through the trees while they were swearing and seemed to be sinking in a lot more. One of them took a shot at me, and I heard the round smack into a tree to my right. I just kept moving to the south, taking whatever paths of least resistance I could see. It was really hard; the trees and plants here are so thick and hard to deal with…after a couple miles I stopped running because I could feel the sweat getting into my undershirt. I tried to take advantage of all the clearings and snowmobile tracks I found. I had no idea where I was, and I didn't want to stop. Eventually though, I did pause long enough to look at my phone and decided to try for the town of Bayview.

"When I started moving after the brief pause, I noticed the cold for the first time. I just had a light jacket and hat, no gloves, and trail runners on my feet, which were getting wet. I kept moving towards Bayview. I knew I could stop and make a call for help on my phone or with the Garmin, but I was afraid I'd freeze to death by the time anyone got there. Then the cold really set in and I was shivering uncontrollably, shaking almost violently and the muscles in my back kept locking up on me. I kept going for a long time, but it got worse and I started to get a little stupid, almost like I was drunk. Eventually I was so fatigued and cold I didn't feel like I could go any further. My brain, in its delusional state, thought I should just crawl into my bivvy under a fallen tree and try to hide there. So that's what I did, and that's the last I remember, until I woke up here on the couch. But I want to thank each of you, you saved my life, and I won't forget it, ever."

Nina, a Captain with the Arizona Department of Public Safety, was the first to speak. "Oh my God, that sounds absolutely harrowing."

"I'll tell you what, I didn't think I'd ever be warm again. To be sitting here next to a fire right now is just the best thing ever."

They talked about the incident some more, then Nina broke the news to Xana that she might be needed to testify in a hearing that was coming up in the next few days. "Vic and I were talking right before the call, and decided it was time for us to make a road trip. So how about if we drive up to Rathdrum and pick you up, say, the day after tomorrow. We'll drive you to Phoenix, and you and I can stay at the AZDPS Training Center while the hearing is going on. Don't worry, we know how to keep witnesses safe, and we don't even know for sure if you'll have to testify."

"Sounds good to me," said Xana. "It will be nice to see you both again."

Vic and Nina said goodbye, then Doc gave Xana one more checkup. He said she looked almost normal but told Jake to call him if anything came up. The three made plans to make a drive in the morning to check Talache Road for Xana's 4Runner, and Doc left.

A minute after he left, Luna came out from hiding and jumped up on the couch next to Xana, looking at her expectantly.

"That's Luna. She just wants you to pet her," said Jake.

"I've never been around cats very much," Xana answered, but petted Luna experimentally a few times as Luna lay next to her, purring. "Wow, this is surprisingly peaceful and relaxing."

"Some people say cats can tell when people are having a hard time and will try to help them. I'm actually in that camp, myself. But Doc's orders are to feed you as much as you can hold, are you ready for more?'

"Yes, I'm so hungry right now, thank you."

Jake prepared more food for her and was surprised at how much of it she could eat. It was almost nine o'clock when she finished, and he could tell she looked tired and ready to sleep. He gave her the option of sleeping on the couch or in his second bedroom. She chose the couch with Luna and the fire. Jake stoked the fire so that it would burn until morning, retrieved her pistol from the truck and gave it to her, and they said goodnight.

Xana had verbally gone along with Jake and Doc's idea to look for her 4Runner in the morning, but she had her own plan.

She'd installed a sophisticated tracking device on her vehicle some time ago. The device served two purposes: To help her find the vehicle while on outdoor excursions, and to help her retrieve it in case of theft. Most of her belongings, as well as a hidden stash of money, were in the 4Runner and she didn't want to lose anything. While in the bathroom earlier, she'd looked at the tracking app on her phone and saw that her vehicle was located at the Preston Security office in Spokane Valley—the same location she'd been spotted at earlier.

Xana knew Jake would likely help her get her vehicle back if she asked, but what she had in mind would be technically illegal and she didn't want to expose him to any risk. She would rather clean up her own mess. Pulling up the Uber app on her phone, she saw that there appeared to be drivers available in the Rathdrum/Post Falls area. Investigating the area further, she found a grocery store in the town of Rathdrum that was open twenty-four hours. She knew what to do, and set the alarm on her phone to vibrate at two a.m.

It seemed like she had just gone to sleep when her alarm woke her. Despite feeling stiff and sore, she got up and put on her trail runners, socks, light coat and hat, as well as her shoulder holster and pistol. The clothing items had all been drying next to the wood stove and were nice and warm. Grabbing her backpack, she went into the bathroom. She found a large towel and stuffed it in the backpack, then eased out the front door, leaving it unlocked. She walked down the long driveway to Boekel Road, then started jogging toward the grocery store. Her spine immediately felt chilled, and it was threatening to lock up on her as it had the day before. The bitter cold, likely close to zero, reminded her of the previous day's discomforts and she felt a tinge of anxiety setting in. She ran harder and knew the grocery store was only about three miles away. The icy road was a dark, lonely ribbon stretching out in front of her, amidst the fields of white snow. When she reached Meyer Road, she turned right and continued running. There was no one else out and about. In another mile she reached Commercial Park

Avenue and turned left, then found the grocery store just a little further ahead.

She bought a box of Clif bars, and chatted up the male clerk as she entered her ride request on the Uber app. She wanted to stay inside as long as she could. The driver was in Post Falls, fifteen minutes away, so she just kept talking to the clerk, who seemed to be more than happy to speak with her. She was used to it and gave him a quick smile when her driver arrived. Her driver turned out to be a surly, middle-aged woman who wasn't talking very much. About a half-hour later, Xana stepped out of the car about a block from the Preston office building. It wasn't any warmer. She quickly walked towards the office, which was surrounded by a barbed-wire fence in a light industrial area. As she drew close, she chose the least conspicuous area of the perimeter and removed the towel from her backpack. After climbing the fence, she threw the towel over the top strands of barbed wire and made it over the top. One of the barbs stabbed her painfully on the left inner thigh, but she kept going and, once on the other side, retrieved the towel and put it back in her backpack while keeping a lookout for humans or dogs. She walked directly to her 4Runner and was relieved to see that it wasn't blocked in by any other vehicles, nor did it seem to be disabled in any way. She opened the driver's door with her keys and entered. The engine started right up, and she glanced briefly behind the driver's seat. It looked like her gear had been gone through but was mostly accounted for, and it didn't look like the inside panel that concealed her money stash had been tampered with. There was a little frost on the windows, but not enough to require any scraping. She drove directly towards the closed front gate—she didn't know if she was triggering any alarms and wanted to get out as quickly as possible. Her front bumper had a brush guard on it, and she positioned the guard right up against the gate and gave the 4Runner some gas. The gate made a disturbingly loud squeal as it gave way and swung to the right, but then she was past it and was driving out of the area. She drove straight back to Jake's house, where she turned off her lights and crept slowly up the driveway. She parked next to the shop building, where her vehicle couldn't be seen from the road, and was back on the couch with Luna and sleeping again by four-thirty.

Jake awoke at seven the next morning and went out to the living room. Xana was awake on the couch and was petting Luna, who looked perfectly content and seemed to have taken a fancy to the visitor.

"Good morning! I usually don't let Luna in my room at night, because she comes and goes so often that it wakes me up. So to have you here is a treat for her, I hope she didn't keep you up or anything."

"Not at all, she's actually very comforting. Now I'm thinking that if I ever settle down, I'm going to have to get a cat as well. Did you name her Luna because she's gray like the moon?"

"Well...my wife named her that, a long time ago."

She saw a look of infinite sadness cross his face. She looked at his left hand, but didn't see a wedding ring. It couldn't have been good, whatever it was. "I'm sorry," she said.

"It's okay. Are you hungry?"

"You wouldn't think so after how much I had last night, but yeah I am."

"I'll get something going."

In just a few minutes he had some food and coffee ready for them at the table, and they sat down to eat. They were silent for a few minutes, then Xana spoke up.

"I need to let you know that we don't need to go and look for my 4Runner this morning. I went and got it last night, and it's right outside by your shop."

"You—how on earth did you do that?"

She explained how she had done it, leaving nothing out.

"You are a very surprising woman. So, after nearly dying, you left here at dark-thirty and jogged over to catch an Uber at the grocery store when it was around zero degrees outside?"

"I was questioning my sanity when I felt the cold again, believe me. And I know you would have helped me, Jake, but I'm used to solving my own problems. Plus, I didn't want to wake you up."

"Well, all I can say is, that was pretty badass. And that's a compliment I wouldn't give lightly. I'll text Doc to let him know we won't need him." He used his phone for a moment. "We have all day, and Vic and Nina won't be here until late tomorrow. Is there anything you need to do, or anything we need to get for you?"

"Just one thing. It looked like they went through all the stuff in my 4Runner. I'd like to go through everything and make sure there's nothing I need to fix or replace."

Jake thought for a moment. "Sure. There's a spot in the shop you can pull into, and then we can just leave it inside while you are in Phoenix. I have a furnace in there, so it won't be freezing."

"Sounds perfect."

Xana spent most of the morning inspecting her gear out in the shop and organizing it in the way she was used to. It was all there, and her stash of money was intact. Other than some new scratches on her brush guard, the 4Runner was in good shape. She went inside and took a shower, did her laundry, and felt like she could breathe again. She thought about Jake for a minute. She knew he was an ex-cop, but he seemed young for that and looked to be about her age. What had happened with his wife and career? It didn't seem to her that there was any female influence whatsoever in the house, and she wondered why that was. He was quite handsome, with dark hair and eyes, and his six-foot frame looked athletic, like he was healthy and active. There was a story with him, and she wondered if she would learn it.

CHAPTER 3

After lunch, Xana sat back down on the couch and Jake sat in a chair nearby. They talked about Vic and Nina for a bit, then Xana's curiosity got the better of her. She folded her legs under herself and looked him in the eye.

"Tell me about yourself, Jake."

Jake pursed his lips for a moment, met her gaze, and nodded. He told her about growing up in northern Idaho, going to high school and college, and getting hired at the Yakima Police Department where he'd met Vic and Doc. He also told her how he'd met his wife, their marriage, and having a son. She could see in his eyes a trace of the happiness that must have filled his life back then. His eyes changed as he told her of the death of his wife and son, followed quickly by the death of his parents, and how he'd retired early and moved back to his home state. Xana felt his sadness filling the room as he spoke, and she sensed he'd been gripped by inertia since returning to Idaho.

He asked her to talk about herself, and she considered her answer carefully. In her old days of being a seductress for the cartel, she realized, someone like Jake would have been considered a prime candidate for her attention. She had no interest in being fake or manipulative with him and cautioned herself to keep their interactions dialed down. She decided to be honest and to simply tell her story, much as she had with Nina a few months ago.

"I was born in Mexico City. My mother came from a good family but was not herself a good person—she was an alcoholic and probably a drug addict as well. She would leave for days at a time, and I learned to hoard food and money to survive. When she was home there was a steady procession of strange men and, when I was around thirteen years old, she thought some of the men were paying too much attention to me and not enough to her. I was sent to live with my aunt and uncle, which turned out to be a good thing and I loved them both very much. Things were fine until right after I graduated from high school, when I learned my uncle had borrowed some money from the cartel—money he was not able to pay back. They beat him, and I was taken as collateral for the loan. The loan was never paid off, so I was basically a slave to an evil man and his wife for several years. I was raped constantly be the man, sometimes by the wife as well, and I had to do all the cooking and cleaning around the house. Eventually I was moved to Phoenix, but I wasn't free. It was clear that if I tried to leave the cartel they would kill me, as well as my aunt and uncle. I was forced to be a seductress for the cartel: They would assign men, and sometimes women, for me to seduce and extract information from. I became quite good at it, but my spirit and my soul were fading away.

"I began to have an inkling of how to escape when I met Nina. I had been sent to her as a fake informant regarding human trafficking, but really my job was to set her up to be killed. Nina was so real and genuine, and in her I saw someone I may have been able to be in different circumstances. At about the same time I learned the cartel had already killed my uncle, and that my aunt was near death from cancer. I saw my chance and told Nina the truth. I told her my whole story, just as I'm telling you now. I agreed to cooperate with her, and many members of the cartel were ultimately arrested as a result. But I'm in a sort of limbo while the court cases play out. The cartel is hunting me, hoping to kill me before I can testify—so I've been a moving target, trying to stay alive until then. I try to stay in shape, and while I was in Colorado I took a lot of firearms courses to be able to protect myself. Along the way I've become very close to Nina, and she and I now consider ourselves to be sisters. We've saved each other's lives a couple times now, and there's nothing I wouldn't do for her or Vic."

Jake told her what was on his mind. "You are a hero. I'm beginning to understand why Vic and Nina hold you in such high regard."

"Thanks Jake. I don't see myself as a hero, but I am determined to survive, I can promise you that." She paused. "And please don't feel sorry for me, I don't want to be pitied and I'm not a victim anymore. I won't burden you with details, but I have taken steps to free my mind as well as my body from the cartel. And the man who raped me for so many years? Well, he and his wife are both in the ground now, never to rape again."

Jake wasn't sure what to say to that. Instead, he asked her how her mother decided to name her Xana.

"As I understand it, the name Xana refers to an ancient, mythical female entity from northern Spain. In mythology, Xana was mostly kind but could be mischievous or even violent if provoked.

Strange as it is, I've been aspiring to those qualities since I left the cartel. So maybe giving me that name was one of the few good things my mother did. I haven't had any contact with her since I went to live with my aunt and uncle. She never called or checked in on me a single time, didn't go to my graduation, nothing. I've mentally shut the door to her, and I have no idea if she's even still alive."

When Jake went to bed that night, he tried to sort out his thoughts about Xana. When he thought about the last few years of his life, it was amazing to him that he currently had a beautiful woman of his own age sleeping just a few yards away. She was clearly an impressive person and he was attracted to her, both physically and emotionally. She was fit, slim, and had a beauty that was both dark and sensuous, along with a confident, easy personality. When he thought of his wife, though, he felt guilty. He had an imaginary conversation with his wife and tried to think of what she would tell him about Xana if she could—after a few minutes, his wife's words came to him: Go slow and be careful but remember to live your life. And be very gentle with this woman; she's opened up to you about her past and that's a big deal. Don't ever betray the trust she's shown in you.

The next day was a busy one for Jake. It snowed overnight, so he had to plow his driveway in anticipation of Vic and Nina's arrival, and he'd invited Doc and his wife over for dinner as well. Then, after he made sure the second bedroom was in good shape, he and Xana prepared a meal for everyone that was ready by the time the four guests pulled up next to the house. He went outside to help Vic and Nina with their bags and got everyone quickly inside the house where it was warm. Nina and Xana had an emotional reunion, then Vic introduced Jake to Nina. He found her to be very pretty and smart, and he sensed she was an excellent cop as well.

Once dinner was served, Doc and his wife entertained everyone with their stories of a cranky neighbor. During a lull in the conversation, Nina looked over at Xana. "It's so good to see you, we were really worried about you."

"Well, I was getting worried about myself too! But thanks again to all of you. Were it not for you, I'd be a popsicle right now."

Jake took the opportunity to tell the visitors about how Xana had retrieved her 4Runner.

"That sounds like Xana," Nina agreed.

Early the next morning the three were up early to begin the trip back south. Jake walked them out to Vic's 4Runner and said goodbye to Vic and Nina as they were getting inside. Outside the vehicle's back door, he and Xana embraced for a moment. She smiled at him, told him she would see him soon, and climbed in. Jake stood outside as Vic drove down the driveway and turned onto Boekel Road. He went back into the house, and it was lonely.

The next day, Jake woke up thinking about something that rarely crossed his mind: Clothing. He'd noticed at dinner that everyone had nice jeans, shirts, shoes, and jackets to wear. By comparison, all his stuff was many years old and looked a little rough. He perused his closet and immediately saw the garment bags in the corner that held his suits—suits he'd worn to funerals. He put that thought out of his mind and looked at the other things he had. Some of it was okay, but most of it had seen better days. He put on his best-looking old clothes and drove to a large department store in Spokane Valley. He didn't like shopping for clothes but was making an exception: He wanted to look better the next time Xana saw him. A pretty and professional lady named Melanie approached him—he introduced himself and warned her that he was going to buy a lot and that she'd be stuck with him for a while. She didn't mind in the slightest and proved to be quite helpful. A couple of hours later Jake had a shopping cart loaded with all new items. They were walking toward the checkout counter when he remembered the gym and mentioned that to Melanie. That stopped her in her tracks.

"And what is it that you wear to the gym?" she asked.

"Well, I just have some old stuff…"

"Follow me."

They loaded down a second cart with workout shoes and pants, shorts, t-shirts, and a couple of hoodies. After Jake paid for everything, Melanie gave him a card.

"This is my friend Melissa, she's a stylist and has a shop close to here. I think you should go see her. Tell her I said "eyebrows". And Jake, if a girl is the reason you are buying all this, I really hope it works out for you. If not, maybe you can come back and see me sometime." She gave him a smile that was quite alluring.

"You are awesome. I'll keep that in mind." She helped him load his shopping bags into his truck and he drove home, thinking about the interesting things that happened when he was not just holed up in his house. When he got home, he looked at his eyebrows in the mirror, wondering what was wrong with them. He didn't think they were too bad, but they were bushy. Definitely bushy.

A couple days later, he met Melissa at her shop. She was another nice lady, married and still marvelous. She asked who had been cutting his hair, and he told her he'd been doing it himself for a few years.

"Well, you've gotten pretty good at it, but I think we can improve in a few ways. Let me show you."

She gave him a cut he was happy with, then showed him how to trim his eyebrows with a long comb and some small scissors.

She sold him a little pair of scissors and some tinted sunscreen as he was paying.

When he got home, he looked at himself in the mirror with his new hair and clothing. He figured the ladies had probably upsold him a little bit. But he also had to admit they'd really helped him out.

In Phoenix, Nina Vasquez was enduring a part of her job she liked the least: a long court process. She was a Captain with the Arizona Department of Public Safety and had been the driving force behind a large federal wiretap case from just a few months ago. She'd teamed up with many federal agencies to get the case moving, and it had been a success: Many cartel members were arrested, and many victims of human trafficking had been rescued. The federal bench in Phoenix was set to hear a combined motion by all defense attorneys involved to suppress evidence the wiretap had produced. This was a normal occurrence following a wiretap and the defense attorneys were giving it their best shot. If they could get the wiretap suppressed, their clients would most likely go free. If they lost, they knew it would be time to start negotiating plea agreements with the U.S. Attorney's Office, because their clients would be screwed. It was extremely difficult to come up with a defense for a client who was on an audio or video recording, plotting to commit federal crimes.

Nina was a lifelong Arizona resident and former college basketball standout. After graduation, she and her husband both joined the AZDPS and had not looked back. As the years went by, Nina studied hard for promotional exams and did very well. Her husband was a good cop but was not as motivated as she was. Unfortunately, he had trouble handling her comparative success and they ended up divorcing. Nina was happily single until she met Vic—they'd been through a lot together and were now nearly inseparable.

Nina and the other law enforcement officers, as well as the U.S. Attorney, had a great feeling about their chances of overcoming the motion to suppress the wiretap evidence. The case had been a little rushed in the beginning, but it was based on solid evidence and a clear pattern of obvious lawbreaking. The U.S. Attorney had asked Nina to have Xana on standby in case she was needed to testify as a direct witness to some aspects of the cartel's activity. Nina agreed to the request, but in turn had asked that Xana be produced only if absolutely necessary.

As it turned out, the motion to suppress the wiretap evidence was postponed. The defense attorneys argued they needed a three-month continuance in order to properly represent their clients. Some of them, no doubt, were sincere about that. Others, knowing the cartel had an almost unlimited supply of funds, inwardly rejoiced at the opportunity to avail themselves of dozens more billable hours. The judge, meanwhile, had not been too happy about having the monster case land on his docket in the first place and was glad to kick the whole thing down the road.

After some discussion with Nina and Vic, Xana decided to fly back up to the Northwest—but to fly into the Tri-Cities airport in Washington State instead of the Spokane airport. The Tri-Cities airport was only about three hours from Jake's house, and there was much less chance of her running into anyone from Preston Security there.

CHAPTER 4

Things had never been easy for Bryan Mitchell, the owner of Preston Security. He'd had to fight for everything he had and then, quite often, had to fight again to keep it all. He came from a hardscrabble background and learned early to use his fists to solve arguments. With his looming size, deep voice, and unquenchable drive to win at all costs, he'd bulldozed his way through childhood and his young adult years. While in his early twenties he'd tried very hard to be hired as a police officer. However, the required psychological and polygraph exams, coupled with a couple of assault arrests, made that impossible and after a few tries he gave up. He settled for a job as a security officer with a large company. He liked the work in general but chafed under some of the policies he saw as stupidly restrictive, particularly when it came to how much force he could use against people who were not obeying his commands. After a few years and some disciplinary trouble, he left the company to start his own outfit.

Preston Security, named after an ornery grandfather who'd help raise him, was the result. His vision of the company was for a reactive, no-nonsense organization that provided top value to his clients. If Preston Security were guarding a building, for example, there would be no waiting for the police if someone was trying to break in. If Preston Security were keeping the peace at a nightclub, individuals who had overstayed their welcome would only receive one warning before feeling some pain. He saw Preston as being a sort of security company on steroids, something which, not coincidentally, could also be said about Bryan and many of his employees.

In the beginning, Bryan wasn't the best manager of his company's finances. Businesses simply weren't willing to spend a lot on security, even for the enhanced security Bryan imagined his company was able to provide. He started selling steroids and performance enhancers to some of his buddies at the gym to bring in a little extra cash. His supplier could get him small quantities of meth as well, so he added the drug to his inventory. Spokane did not seem to have a shortage of meth users, and his business increased. Between the drug sales and the legitimate security jobs he was able to get, Bryan was financially successful within six months. After a year, he was able to bypass his drug supplier and began dealing directly with a man who was part of the Manzanillo cartel—he ditched his small illegal steroid business and concentrated on the more-profitable meth business. Within eighteen months, he was selling fentanyl as well as meth, and business was good.

Preston Security was essentially divided into two branches. One branch consisted of actual security guards, while the other consisted of his drug dealers. Bryan figured out early how to create bogus invoices for security services, and how to launder money with the fake invoices and made-up expense reports. He kept himself a few steps removed from the actual handling of the drugs and made sure everyone knew that snitches would pay the ultimate price for betrayal. He'd already killed two people—with the help of a backhoe, he'd planted them deep underground in the woods north of Spokane.

On the security side, Bryan made sure his officers were feared and respected around town. He tended to hire gym-rat types who didn't put up with anyone's nonsense. Twice, people had tried to sue Preston for assault, but both cases were withdrawn after the victims were subsequently hospitalized with severe injuries. "A broken jaw can't talk," was one of Bryan's favorite expressions.

Bryan made sure to stay in the good graces of his cartel connection, who supplied him with an unlimited supply of meth and fentanyl at a good price. At one point his connection had asked him to keep an eye out for a girl named "Xana" who the cartel wanted to eliminate, and a blurry photo of her was provided. It was made clear that a two-million-dollar reward would be paid to whoever could capture or kill her. And so, on a cold mid-day when a female matching the general description had been spotted loitering outside the Preston office, Bryan and his crew had quickly sprung into action. The woman outside did indeed seem to be the woman in the photo. They were dumbfounded when the woman escaped from them, leaving them with only her vehicle. They towed the 4Runner back to their office, believing they could find documents inside that would enable them to track her down, though they had serious doubts she could survive for long in the woods.

The crew spent several hours going through the items in the 4Runner but were ultimately disappointed to realize there was no paperwork inside whatsoever. The registration for the vehicle was obtained from a Department of Licensing contact, but it listed a generic business and a post office box in Phoenix. They threw a tarp on the frozen ground next to the vehicle and checked each item once again, going over everything carefully and throwing it on the tarp when finished. There was nothing. Nothing, that is, except for a single dry-cleaning tag stapled to the edge of a woman's blouse. The tag was removed, all items were placed back in the vehicle, and the officers retired to their office where they contemplated the single bit of evidence they had. They decided to use some of their contacts the next day to try to determine the source of the tag, and they all went home.

Bryan howled with rage early the next morning when he was notified that the office's perimeter alarm had been triggered, the 4Runner taken, and the front gate broken. He made his entire security division report in, though it was only four a.m. When everyone was present he berated them all for a while, though he knew at some level the lapse had been mostly his fault. In Bryan's mind, Preston Security did things to other people; other people did not do things to Preston Security. Once he calmed down, he led a brainstorming session about how the tag might be identified. One of his officers had the thought of posting the tag on a nationwide blog often used in the security industry. It was an excellent idea. Within a couple of days, the tag manufacturer had been identified. The tag manufacturer, believing they were assisting with a legitimate investigation, provided the name of the specific dry cleaner to which the tag sequence had been issued. The dry cleaner turned out to be in Ft. Collins, Colorado, and a little further investigation showed it was owned by a single, middle-aged, divorced male. On a hunch, Bryan sent one of his attractive female security officers to contact the owner. It took her only one evening to acquire the name of the customer from the owner.

One of Bryan's former officers had been hired at TSA within the past year. Bryan contacted him and asked for help with the name given by the owner of the dry cleaner—cash was exchanged, and the TSA agent found an Arizona driver's license associated with the name. A defunct address was listed on the license. Bryan asked the agent to conduct a daily check of TSA records, and to notify him immediately if the name was used by any passengers, anywhere.

CHAPTER 5

Jake was with Doc in the den of his Coeur d'Alene home, looking at a satellite photo of the Tri-Cities Airport as they developed a plan to get Xana back to Jake's house. Vic and Nina had already completed their plan to get her safely onto the plane and had cautioned Jake and Doc to be prepared for any eventuality. A flight with an arrival time of mid-morning on a Wednesday had been selected, to minimize the number of travelers who would be present. Xana would be flying with a single checked bag, inside which would be a lockbox containing her Sig P365, two magazines, and a box of 9mm duty ammo. Vic told them not to worry about Xana's ability to shoot under stress—he'd seen her in action and had no reservations whatsoever.

After some discussion, they decided on a relatively simple plan. They would take two vehicles from Idaho to the airport: Jake in his Tundra, and Doc in his G-wagon. Jake would park along the north edge of the parking lot and Doc would find a position nearby that would give him a good field of fire covering the airport's main doors as well as Jake's vehicle. Once they arrived, Jake, armed with his Glock 19, would enter the airport. Doc would remain outside, keeping an eye out for suspicious vehicles and with his BCM AR-15 handy. When Xana disembarked, Jake would guard her while she retrieved her bag. Once she had her bag she would go into a stall in the women's room, load her magazines, and emerge armed with her Sig in its shoulder holster. Jake would call Doc to make sure everything looked good out in the lot and would remain on the phone with him as he and Xana walked to Jake's truck. They would walk through the lot a short distance apart, while staying amidst parked vehicles to have cover available if needed.

They thought it was a simple, workable plan.

"A little bit like our old SWAT days, huh," said Jake.

"Yep," replied Doc. "And let's remember the old saying, that SWAT dogs never die."

"That's right. One last thing, let's wear our soft body armor that we used to use under our uniform shirts. I have an extra set I can bring for Xana and it's wintertime, so no one will notice a little extra bulk."

"Good plan."

On the day of Xana's flight, Jake and Doc arrived at the airport about an hour early. Jake waited in his truck while Doc went in to use the restroom, then Jake went in to do the same, carrying the body armor for Xana in a shopping bag. He found a seat in the non-secure waiting area and looked around slowly. Everything appeared to be normal, even a little boring.

The inbound plane arrived a few minutes early, and Jake was there to greet Xana as she walked into the unsecured area. They hugged for a moment, and he was taken aback at how athletic, fit, and beautiful she was, even with no makeup and a plain hairstyle. They talked about her flight, and about how Vic and Nina were doing as they waited for her bag. When it arrived, she went into the women's room and exited a short time later, armed and ready to go with body armor under her shirt. She knew the security plan, but they discussed it once again to make sure they were on the same page, then Jake called Doc.

"How are things looking out there, Doc?"

"It all looks normal, with one exception. There's a white minivan a few rows to the south of me that I saw some movement in the back of earlier, though there's no one in the driver's seat. I'm keeping an eye on it but haven't seen anything else. Let's wait ten minutes to let some of the foot traffic from the flight clear out and I'll keep watching."

"Okay, let's do that, and we might as well just both stay on the phone for now." He explained to Xana what was going on. They reminded each other to keep their jackets open to allow for quick access to their weapons. "Stay off to my right," he told her. "If anything happens, you take the targets on the right and I'll take those on the left." She nodded, and didn't seem concerned in the slightest. After ten minutes, Doc was back on the phone.

"All right, well I haven't seen anything else in the van, so let's do this."

"Okay, we're heading out the doors now."

They walked to the parking lot without incident and began threading their way through the parked cars, with Xana about two car widths to his right. When they were a little more than halfway to Jake's truck Doc started talking to him, sounding a little stressed.

"Heads up, that van is starting up and there's a big White dude in a black jacket in the driver's seat."

"Okay, keep me posted." He informed Xana of the van.

"Watch out now, it's moving," said Doc.

There was a screech of tires, and Jake saw the van quickly approaching he and Xana from the left, only one parking row in front of them. He jammed the phone in his coat pocket and drew his pistol, while noticing that Xana had let go of her bag and was drawing her weapon as well. There was another screech of tires, and the van abruptly stopped in front of them. The van's passenger rear sliding door opened and two men with pistols jumped out—they were just beginning to raise their weapons when Jake and Xana each took one down with multiple shots. As that was happening, Jake saw the driver coming around the back of the van with a raised pistol that was coughing fire. He took a shot at the man, but his aim was off for some reason—then he heard Doc's AR open up and the man fell to the side as if he had taken an axe to the head. Xana was dancing closer to him to get a shot and she gave the man one more bullet as he was falling.

Jake had a funny feeling in his guts and he had to kneel down. Then he fell to the side, his pistol clattering to the ground. The feeling in his guts turned into intense pain and he felt a strange pressure in his lower abdomen. He ended up on his back, looking up at the sky. His mind faltered, and for a moment he thought he could see his son up in the sky. Then a woman's face appeared in front of him, telling him something...he recognized her, though he couldn't remember her name. But it was the face of an angel.

CHAPTER 6

Jake awoke with no idea where he was, or what was going on.

"Where the fuck am I?" he asked of no one in particular. He looked around and saw Doc, sitting in a chair beside him.

"I'll give you a minute to wake up all the way before I explain everything. For now, can you tell me how you are feeling? You've been out for a couple days."

"Like I've got the worst gut ache ever." He looked around. "Where's Xana, is she okay?"

"She's fine. We each got a hotel room across the street and we're taking turns being with you, twelve hours on and twelve hours off. She'll be here for her turn in just a couple hours."

"And my truck?"

"It's right over in the hotel parking lot."

"Shit, I need to leave so I can go feed Luna if I've been here that long!"

"Relax, remember that I have a key to your place—my wife has been visiting her every day and taking good care of her."

"Thank God. Well, please tell her I said thanks, it's a huge relief. I'm feeling awake now, go ahead and give it to me straight. I remember Xana and I shooting the two passengers, then you and Xana shooting the driver, who was shooting me. Beyond that is a blank."

"I'll give you the short version. You were shot twice. One round was stopped by your vest, near your solar plexus. The second was much lower, and it struck the bottom inch or two of your vest on the left side. The vest slowed and deformed the hollow point, but the round still squirted around the bottom of it and went into your abdomen. It went all the way through and was stopped by the back panel of your vest. Because it was deformed, it didn't do quite as much damage as a hollow point normally would. But it still perforated some of your intestines and clipped a couple of blood vessels—the bleeding was the biggest problem. But between me, the ambulance, and the surgeons, we managed to pull you through. As long as nothing gets infected, you should make a full recovery."

"Okay, thank you. I have a feeling that if you hadn't been there, I wouldn't be doing nearly as well. When can I expect to go home, and what's going on with the police investigation?"

"Xana and I have already given statements, and I'm sure they'll be by to see you, now that you are up. The whole thing is on the video of the airport parking lot, so it's pretty apparent what happened. And no surprise—the three dead guys worked for Preston Security. As for when you can go home, maybe in a day or two. They are going to want to see you up and about, so the next step is to get you moving. And of course, you'll have to be checked a few times by your doctor over in Idaho."

A nurse came in and removed his IV and heart monitors, then he took a shot at standing up. He grimaced as he used his abs to stand but made it to the bathroom and then back to the bed. After a few minutes, he stood up and walked up and down the hallway a couple times. His abs felt like he was blowing gaskets and ripping things that shouldn't be ripped, but Doc told him it was normal and to go slow. After a couple hours, Xana arrived for the next shift and Doc went back to his hotel room. Her shift encompassed most of the night hours, but he still tried to walk the hallway every hour or so, with Xana right beside him. Along the way they had some good conversation, but eventually they both got drowsy and went to sleep—he in the hospital bed, and she in the chair next to it.

Xana wasn't at all sure what to think or what to do about Jake. Except for a couple of silly flings in high school, she'd never had a normal relationship with a man, one that she pursued because it was something she wanted to do. Instead, her experiences with men had all been directed by the cartel or forced upon her. She'd only been free from the cartel for a few months, and the thought of becoming involved in a normal relationship had not crossed her mind...until she met Jake. She acknowledged feeling attracted to him on a few levels, and she trusted him, but she also figured it was hopeless to even consider taking things any further with him. She told herself she would help him recover, both in the hospital and at his house, but that she would leave once she was sure he would be okay without her. She'd only begun to process everything that happened to her and knew it wouldn't be fair to Jake to presume she could be a normal woman in a normal relationship. She was already seeing signs of attachment in his eyes, and she regretted that she couldn't leave him sooner before his thoughts went too far.

After another day in the hospital Jake was released to go home, and he and Xana drove back to Rathdrum in his Tundra. She'd told him she would stay for a few days to help him out before she went back on the road. Jake hoped he could convince her to stay longer, but he was detecting a certain hesitancy in her behavior with him, as if she wanted to keep him at arm's length. Still, they had some great conversation and seemed to have many things in common. He had no idea what to think. He was healing well, and the day she had set to leave was approaching all too quickly. The night before she was going to leave, he initiated a direct conversation with her about when they might be able to see each other again. She told him about her thoughts and hesitancies as honestly and softly as she could, which he didn't like hearing but knew he had to accept. Her words were logical, sensible, and only she could judge what was right for her. There wasn't much else he could do. But his instincts and his guts told him there was something they had, something more primitive than rational, that couldn't be just talked away or dissipated with words. Was he being foolish? He had to admit the passing of his wife and his years alone were likely warping his thoughts and emotions. He recalled his wife's admonition to him to go slow and be gentle with Xana. He was, he reflected, quite a mess, both physically and emotionally.

The next morning, they were mostly quiet as they had breakfast, then she gathered her things to leave. Jake's mood was intense as he tried to think of the best way to say goodbye to her. It wasn't easy. As she was at the door to leave, the possibility that he'd never see her again was hitting him hard and he decided, if that was the case, that he was damn sure going to give her a goodbye she'd never forget. The Cowboy Junkies' version of "Sweet Jane" was playing on his sound system—it was his favorite song, and he took it as a good omen. He walked up to her and touched her cheek with his fingertips, then brushed her lower lip with the second knuckle of his index finger. He started to kiss her, with his hands on her shoulder blades. She responded with more passion than her words the day before would have foretold, and his hands slid down to the small of her back, pulling her in tight and melding her body to his. He kissed her with an intensity born of five years of loneliness and heartbreak, of unending pain and fury, and of a broken heart trying desperately to heal. As hard as he kissed her, she kissed him back harder and with a craving that matched his own, entwining her fingers in his hair and pulling him closer yet to her. She kissed him with the exquisite agony of a ruined life, of a heart that didn't trust itself to feel, and of all the times she'd been used by people she hated. In the midst of it all she bit him hard on the neck and on the lip. Finally they separated, breathing hard.

"Call it what you want," said Jake. "But that was real. As real as it gets."

"It was. It was the most real I've ever been with a man. And it's why I have to leave."

With tears in her eyes, she brushed some blood from his cheek with her sleeve, whispered goodbye with a shaking breath, and was gone.

CHAPTER 7

Vic moved boxes around in his closet, trying to find the one he needed. After a couple tries, he thought he had the right one and took it out to his kitchen counter where the light was better—he cut the packing tape with a utility knife and opened the box flaps. On top were a few T-shirts he used to wear under his uniform shirt in the summertime. Underneath the T-shirts were a few sets of thin long underwear for the wintertime and, at the very bottom of the box, was a beat-to-shit black leather jacket, which he removed and laid out on the countertop.

It brought back a flood of memories. He'd purchased the jacket at a secondhand store in the Fremont District of Seattle while still in college. It had been his constant companion for a few years, then he started wearing different jackets when he was a cop. Once assigned to narcotics work, however, the jacket was called back to duty to be worn for many of his undercover operations. He'd begun to consider it to almost be a good luck charm, even though he didn't really believe in good luck charms. Now, many years later, he pulled the jacket on again—it still fit very well, though the shoulders seemed to be a little tighter. It still had the perfect amount of slack around his abdomen. Taking the jacket back off, he shook it out and hung it in his closet, then closed the box and put it back with the others.

Vic had worked at the Yakima Police Department for thirty years and retired as a captain. He and his wife had moved to Las Vegas after he retired, but their marriage had ended in divorce just a year or two ago. Vic had not wanted the divorce and had turned to the 800-mile-long Arizona Trail to find some peace. His long hike didn't end very peacefully—he'd been forced to shoot and kill a cartel member who'd kidnapped a young girl. However, he'd met the beautiful AZDPS Captain Nina Vasquez while in the process of turning the young girl over to authorities and now he and Nina were very close. They'd had to endure several violent attacks from the cartel, but the incidents seemed to have helped give them a powerful bond, stronger than either of them had experienced. A complex state/federal investigation had resulted in the arrests of many cartel members, and Vic and Nina were hoping that things would settle down for them.

Vic was not happy to hear about the trouble that Jake and Xana were having with the cartel-affiliated Preston Security outfit up in Spokane. If there were any two people in the world who had been through enough heartache and grief, he believed, it was Jake and Xana. He knew the current Group Supervisor of the Spokane DEA office as the two had worked together on several eastern Washington cases back in the day. He called the Group Supervisor, also known as the GS, to talk about how he might be able to help the DEA investigate Preston. The two had a long discussion, a discussion which yielded a surprising result: Vic was going back undercover.

As it turned out, the DEA had a good working knowledge of how Bryan Mitchell was running drugs at Preston, but didn't have informants who could make drug purchases from anyone in the organization. With nothing really to lose, the GS agreed to sign Vic up as an informant and let him poke around one of the shady Spokane bars where the lowest-level Preston dealers hung out. The DEA agreed to pay for Vic's transportation to and from Phoenix, and to provide him with a rental car and hotel room while he was in Spokane working with them. Vic declined to accept any additional direct payment for his efforts; it just didn't seem right to him. He cancelled his next haircut appointment and began letting his beard grow out. It didn't take long before he felt like he was ready to buy some meth.

A couple of weeks later Vic, wearing his old leather jacket, met up with three agents a few miles east of downtown Spokane. They gave him a phone, which would also act as a wire so that the agents could hear what was going on and respond if necessary. He was given some cash, then they discussed their simple plan: Vic would simply go in, have a beer, and keep an eye out for Jeremy Niles, the man who was supposed to be the Preston supplier for the bar. The bar, called Jack's Place, was a dilapidated old structure not far from Riverfront Park in downtown Spokane. It had a reputation for serving customers who liked their booze but who also liked a little boost to go along with it. If it felt right, Vic would try to make a small buy from Jeremy. If it didn't seem right, he would just leave and they would try for a buy the next time. Jeremy had been arrested numerous times and Vic had memorized his face from the booking photos.

At about eleven-thirty P.M., Vic entered the bar. He was hoping Jeremy would have had a drink or two by then to relax him, but not so much that he wouldn't remember Vic the next time around. He immediately spotted Jeremy sitting at a corner table with another man. He ignored him and went to the bar, where he sat next to a man who looked like a regular—Vic figured he would probably be a drinker as well as a talker. The man was only too happy to accept Vic's offer to buy him a drink, and the two began chatting aimlessly. They had a long conversation about whether Led Zeppelin was a better band than AC/DC, but then had to recalibrate when they remembered the band Boston. Then they had another drawn-out conversation about the Dallas Cowboys, followed by an important question: Which of the two brunettes from Charlie's Angels was hotter, Jaclyn Smith or Kate Jackson? They agreed Jaclyn was more beautiful, but Kate would likely be more fun to go out with. Along the way Vic bought the man another drink and let it slip that his name was Wyatt—he was using the name because he thought the agents would laugh when they heard him trying to buy dope while using the name of a famous lawman. After about an hour, Vic said he had to get going so he could make the long drive back to Seattle and mentioned he surely did wish he had a little something to keep him awake for the drive, something like a twenty of some nice crystal. The man told him to hold his damn horses and waved at Jeremy. Jeremy walked over, looking a little inebriated but still alert.

"Hey Jeremy, this is my friend Wyatt," said Vic's bar mate. "He has to drive to Seattle and just needs a little something to stay awake."

"Maybe just a twenty," said Vic.

Jeremy, without being obvious, showed Vic a tiny, tied off baggie corner which looked like it contained a miniscule amount of meth. He palmed the item until Vic passed him a twenty, then dropped it into Vic's palm. He went back to his table, not having said a word.

"Not the most talkative bugger," commented Vic.

"No, but he's got the goods. If you see him here, he has some, kind of like Old Faithful."

Vic thanked the man and commented that he'd probably be back in a couple weeks for his job. He walked out of the bar and gave Jeremy a quick nod as he passed him. He met up with the agents again and handed the little bit of meth over, as well as the unspent cash he'd been given. They had him sign a quick expenditure memo, and they planned to make another buy in a couple weeks.

"See you soon," said Vic.

"See you soon—Wyatt."

They all thought it was pretty funny.

A couple of weeks later and at about the same hour, Vic walked into the bar again, nodding to Jeremy who was sitting at the same table he'd been at last time. His bar friend was there again, so he took a seat next to him at the bar. Vic was trying to give the impression he wasn't there just to buy meth, that he really just wanted to hang out and the meth purchases were merely an afterthought. His plan was to make one more very small buy, and then to start pushing for larger quantities on his next trip. To keep up his act he had to kill some time, so he started chatting with the man next to him again—the guy had a sense of humor, so Vic didn't mind too much. They complained about the weather for a bit, then began a debate about which 1960's actress was more statuesque: Raquel Welch or Sophia Loren. Vic was solidly in Raquel's camp, while the man thought that Sophia was clearly the winner. They lamented the fact that Raquel and Sophia had never been in a movie together in which they made out with each other a little bit, because such a scene certainly could have won some type of award or at least broken a few box office records. The man allowed that, because he still had a DVD player, if such a movie existed he would own two DVD copies of it—one to watch and one to have as a backup in case anything happened to the first one. Vic found the logic hard to refute. They noticed the female bartender had been listening to their conversation, so they asked her if she would watch the movie if it had been made.

"Fuck yes," she said, and gave them each a free drink in honor of Raquel and Sophia.

A little later Jeremy walked past them on his way to the men's room. When he came back, Vic stopped him. "I have to hit the road again in a bit. Can I get another twenty?"

"No sweat," said Jeremy. They made a quick hand-to-hand deal, and Jeremy returned to his table. The man next to Vic was nodding approvingly.

"At least I know he talks," said Vic.

"I hear you. On the other hand, it wouldn't be good for the dope man to be too chatty. And if I ran with the crowd he runs with, I'd keep my mouth shut too."

There was an opening there, but Vic decided not to take it. He didn't want the man to be considered a witness by the DEA or by prosecutors. He changed the subject and, a few minutes later, stood to leave.

"I'll see you next time around." He met up with the agents, returned to his hotel, and was back in Phoenix the next day.

Before his next buy, Vic met with the DEA GS and a couple of the agents who had been monitoring him at the bar. Everyone felt things were going well and that Vic had established himself as a buyer with Jeremy. However, they also knew they had only scratched the surface of what was going on at Preston and that there was a lot of work yet to be done. The tiny quantities of meth obtained so far were not nearly enough to warrant a federal prosecution, and they wanted to start making some heavy purchases and wrapping up more members of Preston. Vic had an idea.

"How pure is the stuff I've bought so far; do we have a lab report back yet?"

"It's pretty good," answered one of the agents. "It's in the upper fourth of what we are seeing on the streets here."

"Okay good. Well, why don't I just start making larger buys? I'll tell Jeremy I'm involved with the casinos over in western Washington, that his meth is way better than what's normally seen over there, and that I want to start selling like he does. When the quantities get large enough, he'll probably have to turn me over to the person who supplies him. I'll just see how far up the chain I can get. But we'll need more surveillance when I make the buys. Sooner or later, he'll have to go get the amount I want or someone will have to bring it to him. We'll want to see what happens."

It was a common tactic, and they all agreed it was appropriate in this case. That night, Vic went to Jack's Place and spotted Jeremy at his usual table, alone. He figured there was no time like the present, so he walked up and sat across from him. Jeremy looked annoyed.

"Hey man, sorry to barge in. But I've gotta say, that the stuff you have is good, way better than what I've seen over on the west side. I was gonna see if I can get a little more this time, maybe a couple eight balls." An eight ball was slang for an eighth of an ounce. "I think I can turn it around over there and make a few bucks."

Jeremy cocked an eyebrow. "Of course our stuff is better, it's the best out there. But I'm not fronting anything, I'll need the cash."

They agreed on a price, and Jeremy reached into his pocket. It looked to Vic like he was sorting through what he had, probably picking the best two eight balls. They made the exchange, and Jeremy looked at him again.

"Where are you planning on selling that?"

"I sell legit items to a bunch of the casinos over there, souvenirs and things like that. A lot of the casino workers, and their friends, indulge on the side. Maybe I can help them out."

"I see. A good product helps."

"I come over every two weeks. If it works out for me, maybe I'll get a little more next time."

Vic left the table, had a quick chat with his friend at the bar, and then left.

The next time, Vic received permission from the agents to hit Jeremy up for an entire ounce that hadn't been broken down into smaller quantities. They were trying to ask for a quantity that Jeremy would not have on hand, so they could see how he went about getting it. When Vic entered the bar, Jeremy was talking to someone else at his table. Vic waited nearby, then sat down across from Jeremy when the other person had gone.

"Well, how'd that go?" asked Jeremy.

"It was a real hit, and I was sold out in just a couple of days. This time I'd like to get an ounce, but a whole ounce that's not broken down. I've got a good scale and want to break it down myself."

"Quite a dealer you are becoming. I can get that ounce, but it'll take about half an hour for it to get here. And, so you know, an ounce is the max I'm allowed to sell. Any more than that and you'll have to start dealing with my boss."

"Understood." It was good news. "I'll be at the bar until it shows up." He went over and chatted with his friend, trusting that the agents had heard everything that transpired and would be in position to observe the delivery to the bar. It took about forty-five minutes, but then he saw Jeremy go outside. He came back after a moment and nodded at Vic. He went over to the table.

"It took just a little longer. Traffic."

"I understand." They did the exchange, and the ounce felt like a nice little lump in his coat pocket. "I'll see how I make out with this. But I have a feeling I'll be meeting your boss next time." Jeremy nodded, and Vic headed out. When he met up with the agents, they informed him the ounce had been delivered to the bar in a Preston Security truck. It was not a huge surprise; the truck was excellent camouflage for moving drugs around. The agents were able to get a photo of the driver as well and, all in all, it was a nice evening's work.

CHAPTER 8

Back in Phoenix, Vic gave Nina an update of how his infiltration of Preston Security was going.

"Sounds like good progress. And I must say, I'm kind of liking the longer hair and beard on you. Maybe you'll have to keep that around for a while."

"Could be. Hey, how's Xana doing?"

"She's doing okay, I talked to her yesterday. She's spending some time in Texas, just doing her thing. She opened up to me about Jake while we were talking—evidently when she left Rathdrum it was very emotional for both of them. It sounds like she really cares about him, but she has no experience with normal relationships and so she's lost. Now, she doesn't know if she should have left or stayed with him, and she doesn't want to hurt him any more than he's already been hurt. I didn't know what advice to give her, other than to take things slow. If she were a normal woman I'd recommend she get counseling, but she's such a fierce creature that I don't know how that would go. What do you think?"

"Well, put yourself in Jake's shoes for a minute. He's had a tragic life, and he's been living like a monk for the past few years. All of a sudden, he has this beautiful, super-hot, extraordinary woman of his own age staying in his house. Plus, now they've been through stressful situations together in which they've come out on top. Ten out of ten guys would be falling for her, so that's no surprise. Maybe they just need to get together, blow off some steam, and let the chips fall where they may." He thought for a minute. "I hope they both survive, if that happens."

Nina smiled. "I don't think Xana is ready for that, but yeah—they should do a full warm-up if that happens. And warn the neighbors."

"Jake has been living way under his means. He told me once, after his parents died, that he'll never be able to spend the amount of money he has. Yet you've seen how plainly he lives; he never even buys much except for wood and woodworking tools, maybe a firearm here and there. So, I'd love to see Xana, or someone, help him break the chains and start living in the present. He has the means to do so, and he's such a good guy. He deserves it."

A few days later, Vic walked into Jack's Place and sat across from Jeremy. "Things are moving along, but now word is getting out and I'm getting phone calls day and night. It's fucking annoying, how do you keep your sanity?"

"Tweakers are the worst, they will be the death of you if you let them. If I were just starting out I'd get a separate phone for selling, tell everyone what my hours were, and only have the phone on during those hours. Whatever you do, don't let them know where you live or they will come knocking at the worst possible times."

"That's solid advice. So, I've scraped some money together and I have enough to buy four ounces this time. Can we make that happen? I know I have to meet your boss."

"Yeah, that'll be Frank. I'll text him with your order, then you can wait at the bar. He'll want to do it out in the parking lot, he doesn't like to show his face much."

"All right."

Vic looked for his friend, but didn't see him. He sat at the bar and nursed a beer, chatting a bit with the female bartender who was beginning to recognize him as somewhat of a regular. After a while Jeremy caught his eye, and he walked over to him.

"Black Honda Accord, dark windows."

"Got it."

He walked out to the lot, found the Accord, and knocked on the front passenger door window. Vic generally didn't get in cars that had a suspect behind the wheel. Frank, who turned out to be a large, muscular man with intense, suspicious eyes, rolled down the window and they began a discussion through the opening. He asked Vic some pointed questions, particularly about why he was in Spokane if his main business was over in Seattle. Vic explained he had legitimate sales to one of the medium-sized casinos in the Spokane area.

"Well, we don't care about you selling your trinkets there. But don't be selling our product there, that casino is already spoken for."

"Understood, my phone's been ringing enough with what I have going on over on the west side."

Vic negotiated for a better price than what he'd paid for the single ounce, and Frank agreed to cut the total amount slightly. They did the deal, and Frank gave Vic his cell number for future business.

The next morning, Vic attended a meeting at the DEA office with the agents he'd been working with as well as the GS. The agents wanted to get the purchase amount up to at least a pound, to ensure that the U.S. Attorney's office would prosecute the case. Vic felt confident he could get a pound from Frank, but suggested they start talking about what the end game for the case might look like. The agents told him they really wanted to get the owner of Preston Security, Bryan Mitchell, involved in the purchases so that he could be arrested along with Frank and Jeremy. It made perfect sense to Vic, as his goal was still to do as much damage to Preston as possible. They decided to have Vic order up a pound on his next trip and see if Bryan came out of the woodwork at all.

Jake had been neglecting his walnut table project and decided to give it some attention. He wanted the front apron of the table to have a slight curve on its underside—he traced the curve onto the selected board with a set of trammel points attached to a long stick. After cutting the curve on his bandsaw, he cleaned it up with a spokeshave until it was silky smooth. Woodworking was intensely satisfying to him, and it gave his hands something to do so his mind could function at a higher level. Plus, he liked the idea of creating beautiful items that, if properly cared for, would last several lifetimes. It helped him feel at peace when he was in his house, surrounded by things he had built with his own hands.

Lately, however, peace had been difficult to come by. His abdomen still gave him enough pain that he wasn't able to go to the gym and was restricted to light workouts at home. He missed the exertion. Also, his thoughts turned to Xana several times a day, particularly to their last day together before she left. His thoughts tended to be pessimistic about any possible relationship with her, or with any other woman, for that matter. He'd lost his wife in a very painful way and then, after years of being a widower, had begun to see a chance at something with Xana. Now she, too, was gone.

Were his feelings for Xana just a silly infatuation, brought about by simple proximity to her and by going through some stressful circumstances together? He recalled many of their conversations, especially the ones in which she didn't seem to be trying to maintain an emotional distance from him. He'd felt a real connection with her. She'd been honest with him about her past, which he deeply appreciated, and he understood her hesitation about being involved with something normal—if a relationship between the two of them, each with their own traumatic histories, could even be called normal.

But was it possible she simply didn't feel for him the way he felt for her? He knew he'd be a fool to discount that possibility. Maybe he was just destined to be alone. In the meantime, she'd been the one to walk away from him, so he figured it was up to her to reach out if she wanted to see him anymore.

And if he never heard from her again? Well, there were bound to be perfectly nice girls, like Melanie from the department store, who might want to spend time with him. Or, he could just go back to having imaginary conversations with his dead wife.

But what he really wanted was something with Xana. Now that he'd felt the fire, he didn't want to go back to the ashes. And he was throwing off some sparks himself.

CHAPTER 9

It was a good thing, Bryan Mitchell reflected, that he was used to dealing with problems. Sometimes it seemed to him his life had been nothing but one problem to solve after another. So, it didn't surprise him too much when his quest to get two million dollars for killing the crazy Xana girl had sprouted so many difficulties. He'd been seriously annoyed when she escaped his group in the woods the first time. The second time, she not only escaped again but, along with her two buddies, killed three of his best shooters.

Bryan had really hoped to get more information on the three who had killed his men from the state court system, in which he had a couple of good contacts. He was told, however, that because his men had died there were no cases that needed to be brought to court: The killings were considered to be self-defense, and the names were never revealed.

It was all very frustrating, especially because he could really use the money. To keep his employees loyal, he'd paid for the funerals of the three dead men and had made a substantial donation to the surviving families. He'd also been shelling out a lot of overtime payments in efforts to locate Xana—but the efforts had so far produced nothing. As he often did, he leaned heavily on his drug sales to keep himself and his business afloat. He pushed his dealers to hustle a little more and told them to stop being lazy and to find new customers. He'd been pleased to hear that Jeremy and Frank had been selling to a promising new customer from the west side of the state, and he liked the idea of his meth being sold over a larger geographic area. The man had recently bought four ounces and had mentioned a burgeoning sales business on the west side. Bryan had quizzed Jeremy about how the transactions with Wyatt had begun and was satisfied with the explanation. He told Jeremy and Frank that if Wyatt returned to Spokane to buy larger quantities to let him know: He wanted to meet the guy himself and get his own feel for him.

After some discussion, Vic, the Spokane DEA agents, and an Assistant U.S. Attorney agreed on a plan for the next step of their operation. Vic would order up a pound of meth from Frank and ask to talk to Frank's boss about getting a break in the price. If Bryan showed up and had some recorded conversation with Vic about meth sales, the investigation would be considered to have achieved its objective and Bryan, Frank, and Jeremy would be arrested. If Bryan did not appear, Vic would simply buy the pound from Frank, and they would regroup for the next attempt.

On the day of the buy, Vic made a call to Frank from an undercover, recorded phone line at the DEA office. He told Frank he wanted to buy a full pound and that he wanted to have a talk with Frank's boss about getting a price break for future deals. Frank agreed to the pound buy, but seemed hesitant his boss would meet with Vic, and said he'd check and call him back. After an hour Frank called back and said that, as it turned out, his boss had been wanting to meet and would be there at the deal. A meeting time of nine P.M. was set for the parking lot of Jack's Place.

At seven P.M., Vic attended the mission briefing at the DEA office. There were about fifteen DEA agents and local narcotics officers, as well as three uniformed Spokane PD officers who would be responsible for making traffic stops if needed. The game plan was the same as they had discussed—if Bryan showed up and engaged in conversation everyone would be arrested after the buy. If he didn't show up, the pound deal would simply occur, and Frank would be allowed to leave after the sale.

The agents and narcotics officers all knew that as drug deals got larger, there was more chance of the dealers getting cagey and wanting to do things designed to make it difficult for police in case the buyers turned out to be undercover officers. One common tactic was for the dealers to try to make a last-minute change in the location of the buy. The agents and officers agreed that if Frank and Bryan tried that, Vic would not go along with it and would instead suggest the back parking lot of a nearby hotel. If Frank and Bryan didn't want to go there, then the whole deal would be called off. There was always the chance Vic could be set up to be ripped off, and there was no sense in him agreeing to go to a surprise location. The GS made assignments for surveillance of the buy, and for potential arrests at both the parking lot of Jack's Place and the hotel parking lot.

Vic waited until a few minutes past nine o'clock, then pulled into the Jack's Place parking lot in his rental car. He spotted Frank and pulled up next to him, so that the driver's doors were facing each other. They rolled their windows down, and Vic immediately saw the first complication of the night: There was a second man sitting in the front passenger seat of Frank's Accord.

"What's up Frank, and is that your boss next to you?" he asked. He knew it wasn't Bryan because he'd seen a few of Bryan's booking photos, and he recognized the man, from DEA photos, as the one who had driven his first ounce to the bar in the Preston truck.

"Nah, this is just a friend of mine. The boss does want to meet you before our deal though, how about you follow us. He's just down the road a bit."

This triggered a delicate negotiation between Vic and Frank. Vic had to make the case that he trusted Frank, but didn't yet know his boss or the man in the passenger seat and had to take precautions against getting ripped off, or worse. After a few minutes they agreed to meet the boss at the secondary location that was part of the mission plan. Vic drove to the designated parking lot, followed by Frank and his passenger. Once there, they all got out of their vehicles and stood around chatting, waiting. After a few minutes a man Vic recognized as Bryan pulled up in a large, jacked-up pickup with a loud exhaust. Vic noted that Bryan positioned his truck close to and facing an exit, as if to be prepared for a rapid escape.

Vic and Bryan then had a substantive conversation together. Bryan implicated himself explicitly in all areas of drug trafficking as he bragged about his cartel connection, mentioned several times he had fentanyl pills available as well as meth, and even gave Vic tips on packaging to increase sales. He then said he had to get going but exhibited a layer of shrewdness as he instructed Frank to wait fifteen minutes before concluding the deal. Bryan then got back into his truck and left.

This scenario, Vic knew, put the officers in a bit of a bind and had the effect of splitting the available personnel. A few officers would have to follow Bryan until the deal was concluded, to prevent Bryan from notifying Frank if he was stopped before the sale was made. Meanwhile, the officers left with Vic and Frank also wanted to wait until the deal happened, so that the U.S. Attorney's desire to have at least a pound quantity of meth transacted was fulfilled—and they had no way of being sure Frank had the pound with him. It was entirely possible he may have to go somewhere else to pick up the meth.

As it happened, Frank did not have the pound with him and had to go get it. When the fifteen minutes was up, he got in his car and told Vic he'd be right back. His passenger stayed behind with Vic, and the two engaged in some forced small talk until Frank returned about ten minutes later. Finally the exchange was made, and Vic gave a pre-arranged signal to the cover officers. About ten officers and agents immediately moved in for the arrests, and, in keeping with the mission plan, pretended to arrest Vic as well. Vic was placed in the back of the GS's car, and the GS quickly removed the handcuffs from Vic. As he was doing so, he gave Vic some bad news: Bryan had been driving like a maniac after leaving the hotel parking lot, and he had managed to lose the surveillance officers after about ten minutes. The officers had not wanted to drive the way Bryan was driving, to avoid making it obvious they were police officers. Bryan was in the wind.

Agents gave Frank a one-time offer to cooperate with them. He declined and he and the man in the car with him both requested attorneys. Agents had arrested Jeremy at Jack's Place and he, too, requested an attorney. Meanwhile, Frank's phone was blowing up with calls from Bryan, and everyone knew Bryan would quickly figure out what had happened. Agents set up surveillance on his residence but left when Bryan had not returned after a few hours. They notified all surrounding agencies of the probable cause they had for Bryan's arrest and had to content themselves with the knowledge that he would be taken into custody sooner or later.

When Bryan left the hotel parking lot, he'd been convinced that Wyatt was an actual drug dealer and that they had a lucrative future. His instructions to Frank had been part of his usual instructions to his dealers—he tried to keep himself removed in time and location from the hand-to-hand transactions. He thought he'd seen a vehicle pull in behind him rather quickly, and so he drove a little more aggressively than usual and after two or three minutes the car dropped off. After driving another mile, he pulled into a strip mall parking lot and called Frank. It concerned him when there was no immediate answer. Over the next ten minutes he called Frank's phone repeatedly, to no avail. Jeremy wasn't answering his phone either, so he called Jack's Place and asked for Jeremy—the bartender said Jeremy had gone out to the parking lot a long time ago but had never returned. Bryan knew what had happened, and began to look around the parking lot carefully, checking for possible undercover police. He didn't see anything unusual, but a sick feeling was mounting in his guts. Grabbing a pen and paper, he quickly made a handwritten list of the important numbers and email addresses in the contacts section of his cell phone. He then broke the phone enough to allow him to remove the battery, smashed the remainder, and threw the pieces into a nearby garbage can. Getting back on the road, he drove to a Walmart store and made cash purchases of a burner phone, tablet computer, and a few groceries. After a quick stop for fuel, he headed north out of Spokane.

Bryan believed in having a backup place to live, and owned a small house a little to the west of the town of Newport. It was about an hour's drive from Spokane and he drove straight through, making sure to strictly obey all traffic laws. When he arrived, he parked his truck in the garage, though he could barely close the garage door once it was inside. He made some food while he gave the burner phone a charge, then called his sort-of-permanent girlfriend. She was also one of the security officers on the legitimate side of Preston and he trusted her about as much as he trusted anyone, which wasn't all that much. His Newport house had been purchased under her name, so he figured he'd better keep her close and provide her with some benefits for helping him while he figured out what the hell was going on. She'd almost left him a couple months ago, when she found out he'd been utilizing the services of a call girl. He had been sweet-talking her and trying to re-establish their relationship since then—it hadn't been easy and had taken all the limited amount of charm he could muster.

After some conversation, his girlfriend realized his predicament and agreed to help him. She picked up some groceries and supplies, then drove to Newport. When she arrived, she helped him cut off his beard and cut his hair short. Then, they sat down on the couch and tried to come up with a plan that made sense. For the time being they decided she would run the legitimate side of the business, while he would continue to direct the drug side from the Newport house. They both knew that Bryan was likely to lose his security license eventually, but figured they might as well keep making money while they could. His girlfriend would also remove the Preston decals from one of the businesses' white trucks and arrange to get it up to Newport, so Bryan would have something less conspicuous to drive around. They thought it was the best plan for the short term, but didn't know how long it would work. As the night grew late, the realization of the trouble Bryan was in began to weigh on them both, and they grew silent. They went to bed at midnight, but their worries kept them awake long after that.

Back in Phoenix, Vic was glad his biweekly trips to Spokane had come to an end. It was too bad Bryan wasn't yet in custody, but he would be eventually, and his organization would be on its heels. He carefully placed his old leather jacket back into its box, closed the flaps, and taped them back up.

CHAPTER 10

Bryan endured a tough month at his Newport house. It hadn't taken long for word to get out that he was wanted by the police, and his security jobs were drying up quickly. He'd already had to lay off about half of his security officers, and most of those remaining were looking for other work. His girlfriend was sticking with him for the time being and was helping him manage the demise of his business. His drug sales were holding steady, though he had to push his dealers hard after the loss of Frank and Jeremy.

He'd learned the U.S. Attorney's office was going to prosecute Frank, his friend, and Bryan, but they had sent Jeremy's case to be prosecuted by Spokane County since his sales were relatively minimal in quantity. This was good news for Bryan, as he had contacts in the state court system that may be able to give him information from the police reports. The information ultimately provided to him was better than he could have imagined: The reports had background information on Bryan that included the incident at the Tri-Cities airport. The names and addresses of Xana, Jake Connor, and a physician were included in the reports. Bryan recognized the address listed for Xana as being one that Preston had already determined to be defunct. But the addresses for the other two, it appeared, were probably accurate. With his dwindling manpower situation, Bryan felt like he didn't want to act on the information by himself. He called his cartel connection.

Ezequiel "Zeke" Mendoza, the Manzanillo cartel's premier sniper and operator in the U.S., was a careful man who was capable of paying exceptionally close attention to detail. Born in Michoacan, Mexico to a poor family, he'd known from a young age that he wanted something better than what his parents and relatives had. He'd joined the Mexican Marines to get away from farming and hadn't looked back. He thrived in the discipline and regimented lifestyle of the military and began to look forward to the skirmishes his unit had with drug cartels. Zeke's natural skill with firearms did not escape the notice of his superiors, and after just a short time they sent him to a six-month school where he learned to be a sniper.

At the school, Zeke realized he had found his calling. His father had taught him how to shoot from a young age, but the school was light years ahead of anything his father had ever known. Long hours on the range gave him confidence in his ability to hit targets at varying distances in all conditions. But shooting was only a part of the skill needed to be a sniper: The school also taught him to be creative and resourceful in finding ways to get close enough to a target to get a shot—and to get away after taking out a target. The infiltration/exfiltration aspects became his specialty, mostly because of his desire to stay alive long enough to retire and to lead a life which, he imagined, might be a nice change from his time in the military.

Things did not go quite as Zeke planned once he retired. He had a series of unsatisfactory relationships with women, none of whom had any chance or inclination to understand how his mind worked; and he had even less inclination to explain to them what he'd been doing for the majority of his adult life. He was running out of money quickly and was beginning to think he'd have to rejoin his old unit. One day, he had a fortuitous call from another retired marine he'd served with and whom he considered a friend. His friend had been working for the Manzanillo cartel and told him to forget the Marines, that he could make better money and have a better life in the cartel. His friend described life in the cartel in such a way that it overcame Zeke's hesitancy to work for the other side of the law. After all, the Mexican Marines had a reputation of being reliable in the struggle against cartels. But Zeke reasoned he had only one life to live and that maybe it was okay, after all his years of sacrifice, to look out for himself for once.

His abilities impressed the cartel. Time after time, he demonstrated his ability to get in, take the shot, and get out. It wasn't that his techniques were anything elaborate or unusual. On the contrary, his "secret", if he had one, was that he used the simplest methods available and was leery of complicated missions. After a couple years, Zeke was sent to the U.S., where operations were more dangerous and the police responses more professional. He had to up his game considerably—not in the shooting, but in his infil/exfil plans and in covering his tracks while travelling. He was provided with a residence in the Dallas area, which was central to the rest of the U.S. and an area in which his firearms and gear purchases did not raise any eyebrows.

When Zeke received orders to take out Jake Connor, his first action was to review the background information of the target meticulously. He saw that Connor had been a police officer and had a fair amount of SWAT experience. Connor had also been involved in a shooting with three security officers who were trying to cash in on the two-million-dollar reward for Xana. Zeke knew about the reward and had tried to find her himself, though he'd come up empty—the reward was quite an incentive.

It was clear to Zeke why he had been assigned the mission to take out Connor: He was a dangerous man who would be best dealt with from a distance. Further, he lived alone in a house in a rural area, surrounded by fields which, at this time of year, would be covered in snow. Pulling up a satellite image of Connor's property, Zeke noted a shop-sized building, detached from the main house, and he could see tire tracks leading from it. He concluded that Connor had to walk from his house to the shop whenever he left his property. What Zeke wanted was to set up in a location that put the shop mostly between him and the front door of the house: That way Connor would be walking towards him as he left the house, which would make an easier target than if he were walking side-to-side. He studied the surrounding fields and looked for a suitable spot about five hundred yards away from the front door. After noting several possibilities, he felt like he had the beginnings of a plan for the shot.

Next, he turned his attention to his infil/exfil. He much preferred to work alone but saw that in this case it would be best if he had one reliable person helping him. He asked for, and received, permission to use an experienced cartel member who lived in the Spokane area. He called the man, whom he knew slightly from a previous mission, and asked him to make a rush order from a local company for two magnetic vehicle signs advertising a fictional utility company. The man was cautioned to wear a disguise and to pay for the signs with cash. He also told him to rent a generic white double-cab pickup truck for two weeks and to have it ready with the signs as quickly as possible. The only other items Zeke needed were a white sheet and a fluorescent yellow vest, such as a utility worker might wear while out in the field. Once he'd acquired those items, he double checked his usual sniper gear to make sure it was in good shape. He had several rifles to choose from, and for this mission he decided to go with a suppressed Remington 700 model in 6.5 Creedmoor, topped with a Leupold Mark 4 scope. He trusted the Creedmoor round to give him a little advantage in case it was windy.

The next morning, Zeke loaded his gear into his generic Toyota Camry and began the drive to Spokane. The trip took him four days, because he veered west into California to avoid the worst of the winter snow. Once in Spokane, he rented a room and caught up on his sleep. The next morning, he made a drive to Boekel Road on the outskirts of Rathdrum to get a ground-level impression of the terrain. There was a slightly uneven area in one of the fields within his selected zone, about seventy-five yards from the road. It was just a little upheaval in the dirt, with a few rocks piled around it—it would be enough to shield him from view of passing motorists once he had his camouflage in place. Returning to his hotel, he had his accomplice meet him and they discussed the operation. His accomplice had the signs and truck ready to go, and gave Zeke a piece of information he didn't know: Once the hit on Connor had been made and Zeke's exfil was complete, the accomplice had been directed to notify a separate team detailed to go after the physician named in the court documents. Zeke was glad to get that information, and it cemented his plan to be out of Idaho and Washington immediately following Connor's death.

At three o'clock the next morning, Zeke loaded his gear into the accomplice's rented truck in the back lot of his hotel and the two drove to Boekel Road. When they were sure there were no cars nearby the truck pulled over and Zeke got out with his two large duffle bags, about a half mile from the location of his "hide". He didn't want to leave footprints in the snow leading to his hide directly from the road, and so had planned a long, sweeping trek that would mostly leave his footprints out of view. As the truck left him, he quickly walked away from the road to avoid being seen by motorists. His duffle bags were heavy, but they were balanced and the exertion helped keep him warm in the sub-freezing temperatures. There was a quarter moon, and he could see his breath as he walked through the frozen white fields. Only one other car drove past as he walked, and he simply crouched down on the far side of his bags and didn't move until it was gone. When he reached his hide, he stomped around on the snow to get it packed down, then laid a small ground sheet on top of the firm area. He unfolded an insulated sleeping pad and placed it on top of the ground sheet, then added a sleeping quilt that was rated for zero-degree temperatures. After putting on his fluorescent yellow vest, he crawled under the quilt, removed his rifle from a bag, and placed it on the ground sheet in front of him. It was already loaded, and he worked the action to cycle a round into the chamber. He'd already dialed in the turret adjustments for the five-hundred-yard shot. After making sure he had a good view of Connor's front door, he placed his duffle bags on either side of him and then covered himself and all his gear with the white sheet. He tucked the sheet underneath everything to secure it—there was a little wind and he didn't want it flapping around. Zeke felt slightly cold but was not shivering and had the patience of a true sniper as he waited to get a shot. His plan was to watch the house until ten P.M., after which he would get picked up and returned to his hotel for a few hours if he hadn't made the shot. The cycle would repeat itself until the target had been eliminated. While he waited, Zeke watched the house through his scope and made note of which lights were on. At about six-thirty, a couple of interior lights came on and he felt his heart rate start to increase. He made a quick call to his accomplice and gave him an update—the accomplice was staged near a small commercial area and was ready to respond at a moment's notice. At around seven, the sun was rising and Zeke could hear that traffic was picking up significantly on Boekel Road. From time to time he could see shadowy movements inside the house, but the target had yet to emerge. Just before eight fifteen he saw the front door open and his target step outside. He was a little surprised to see that Connor was carrying a rifle case and a duffle bag, very much like the same ones he had on either side of him. He quartered the target's chest in his scope, holding slightly to the left to allow for a little wind coming from that direction. Unexpectedly, the target stopped walking and seemed to be staring right at him. He took the shot.

Jake awoke in a cautiously optimistic mood. He'd been getting out of the house more and had even driven into Coeur d'Alene a couple times to visit his attorney. His abdomen was feeling much less sore and, better yet, he and Xana had been having frequent phone conversations. He found it easy to speak with her over the phone, especially when compared to how he'd felt while counting down the days until she was going to leave his house. There was no pressure, it was smooth and natural, and they'd begun to understand each other a bit more. Best of all, she was planning to visit him in just a matter of weeks. Jake had a quick breakfast, then gathered a few things together for a trip to the range he and Doc had planned for the morning. He walked outside and something was sparking his mind—he realized there was something different about the landscape he'd seen hundreds of times before. As he paused for a better look, he felt a quick sensation of a cruel blow to his sternum. And then there was nothing.

Zeke confirmed that his target was down, then called his accomplice for the pickup. He began moving very quickly: His shot had been suppressed but was far from silent, and he knew a lot of veterans, retired cops, and civilians lived in northern Idaho who would certainly recognize the sound for what it was. He jammed all his items into the two duffle bags and began the seventy-five-yard walk to the road. There were numerous cars driving by, but he kept his head down and trusted the yellow vest to keep suspicions to a minimum. The white truck arrived just before him and he quickly tossed the duffle bags into the back seat, then entered the truck through the front passenger door. No one in the area seemed to be alarmed. His accomplice eased the truck up to speed, and they began taking various backroads, heading roughly south and east towards Coeur d'Alene. It was the opposite direction of where they were ultimately going to go. After a mile or so, they reached out and removed the magnetic door signs from the exterior of the truck. They kept moving, eventually arriving at an entrance to I-90 just west of Coeur d'Alene. They took I-90 back west towards the Spokane hotel Zeke was staying at. Once at the hotel, the accomplice parked near Zeke's Camry and waited while he gathered his items from his room and checked out. Zeke transferred all his gear into the trunk of the Camry and got on the road, heading towards Oregon. It had been a successful operation. Yet he had some unfamiliar regrets and was not happy: He was thinking that, in another life, the man he'd killed could well have been his brother-in-arms.

The man everyone called "Doc" was an interesting character. He'd been raised in Michigan, back in the days when American cars were still mostly being made there. He was quick, smart, and athletic, and in his high school and undergraduate college years he took an interest in martial arts. He studied and received black belts in Karate, Aikido, and Ninjutsu. Later in life, he focused more on brutally effective self-defense systems used by certain special forces units within the U.S. military. As a young man, he took to heart one of the fundamental philosophical lessons put forth by martial arts: The lesson that his fighting skills should only be used for good purposes, and that other people should be safer because of his presence. The idea of helping others be safe was a big part of his motivation for becoming a physician. As time went on Doc settled in Yakima, married a wonderful woman, and had two beautiful daughters. One day he learned of a program offered by the Yakima Police Department: It was called the Reserve Officer program, and it offered civilians the chance to go through an extensive training program and to eventually be commissioned as Reserve Police Officers. Doc was intrigued by the idea, investigated the program, and signed up. It was another chance to help others be safe, and he liked the idea of adding some police skills to his repertoire. His fellow physicians were a little alarmed to hear of this development and many attempted to offer him sage counsel, usually some variation of "You have lost your fucking mind." But Doc was driven to pursue his goals, and over time became the most-qualified sniper on the Yakima SWAT team. His presence as a sniper and as a physician were much appreciated, and there were several times when he was called upon to provide emergency care for officers and suspects. It was in his capacity as a SWAT officer that he met Vic and Jake.

Doc had been trying to call Jake, to ask him to bring a spotting scope to the range with him. He was a little concerned when Jake didn't respond; usually he answered or got back to him right away. He decided to drive out to the range anyway, and figured he'd hear from Jake sooner or later. Doc was always vigilant, but everything that had occurred within the past few weeks had pushed him to be even more so. As he loaded his gear into his G-wagon he removed the rifle he was taking that day, a SCAR 7.62, from its case, inserted a magazine, and placed it on top of the back seat. He opened his garage door and stood just outside his vehicle with one hand on the SCAR as he scanned the neighborhood. Everything looked normal. About fifty yards down the road he saw steam from a running vehicle's exhaust, but that was a common occurrence on a cold morning. He pulled onto the street and drove past the idling vehicle. It was a tan Chevrolet SUV with Washington license plates, and two men he didn't recognize were sitting in front. He made a mental note, then continued driving toward the range. After a quick fuel stop, he was back on the road. He was alarmed to see the SUV he'd seen earlier behind him, and it stuck with him through a couple of turns. His wife was visiting their daughter a few miles from their house, and he called her and told her not to return home until he called her again. The SUV continued to tail him, a few vehicle lengths behind, as he drove on a long, curving road that led to the range. There was no way for him to know for sure that the occupants of the SUV meant him harm, but he developed a plan in his mind to call their bluff and maybe feed them some misinformation. He recalled that the entrance to the range led off to the right, and that across the road from the entrance was a parking lot for a trail that led into the woods. When he had almost reached the range entrance, he signaled for a right turn and saw that the SUV did the same. However, he drove straight past the entrance and, at the last second, pulled into the parking lot for the trail. The driver of the SUV did not react quickly enough to follow him and had to continue down the road. Doc pulled right up to the trailhead, grabbed his SCAR as he exited his G-wagon, and started trotting down the trail at a rapid clip. He knew that the next turnaround opportunity for the SUV was half a mile down the road. The woods were very thick and gave him concealment and cover almost instantly. His maneuver would determine if the occupants of the SUV were after him, and if so, he wanted to be able to choose where the fight would occur. After travelling only a couple hundred yards, he thought he heard a vehicle door close from the area of the parking lot, and he quickened his pace even more. After another few hundred yards he saw a small clearing off to his left—he moved past the clearing for fifty yards, veered off the trail to the left for about twenty yards, then began walking back in the direction of the parking lot. He had set up a classic "J" ambush, and found a spot behind a large fallen tree trunk to kneel behind as he waited. The clearing gave him a nice view of the trail, and he settled in to watch it from behind the excellent glass that sat atop his SCAR. After just a few minutes, he saw the two men he'd observed in the SUV walking towards him, both with pistols out. They had no police insignia, and he knew they were trying to kill him. He took the one in the back with a chest shot, and then the one in the front less than a second later. He started moving back towards his G-wagon. There was no reason to check the men; he knew where he'd put his bullets and, from the way they'd fallen, he knew they were dead. He wanted to check on Jake, and when he reached his vehicle he tried again to call him but still received no response. He pointed his vehicle towards Rathdrum and drove there as quickly as he could. He grew more fearful for his friend with each passing mile. And then he arrived and found Jake outside his house, dead. It crushed Doc to realize that Jake's body was a cruel metaphor for how his life had been for the past few years: Jake was broken and alone.

CHAPTER 11

Doc was in a daze for several hours as he sat in his vehicle on Jake's property, waiting for the sheriff's office to wrap up their on-scene investigation. When the officers were nearly finished, he called his wife to come pick up Jake's cat. His wife, who loved Luna, responded with a pet carrier but was crying so much she couldn't speak. Doc knew Luna was about to become a permanent member of his household, but he wouldn't have it any other way. In the dark, he and his wife solemnly drove back to their house, and, once close, he had his wife park a few blocks away while he cleared the property. He called her in when he was confident it was safe.

Xana had been driving eastbound on a Texas highway when she got the phone call from Nina. Before Nina even finished her first sentence, Xana took the median at a high rate of speed and was driving toward Idaho. She took the information provided by Nina stoically, and asked her several pointed questions about the circumstances of Jake's death, as well as about what had happened with Doc. By the time she hung up, she had a fairly good idea of what had transpired, and her emotions threatened to take over. She really wanted to pull over somewhere and collapse within herself. She kept driving. She wanted to scream her lungs out, but she just kept driving. Nonetheless, her mental toughness could not keep the tears from her eyes. She cried until her face was a mess and she was out of Kleenex, then she cried some more, just letting the tears roll down into her shirt. She cried for a couple of days, until she was close to Idaho, then finally stopped the tears. She checked into a hotel, slept around the clock, ate a lot of food, and slept some more. She had a lot of questions, but believed she knew where she could find at least some of the answers.

The next morning, Xana rented a minivan and transferred some of her outdoor clothing from her 4Runner into it, as well as a few food items. She'd found Bryan Mitchell's address online—it was in Spokane's affluent South Hill neighborhood. For the next two days, she made several passes of the house in her minivan, at all hours of the day and night. There was never any sign of activity, and there was a placard in the front yard advising the house had a security system. The house was her only means of finding Bryan, and she decided to make entry into the house the following night to see if she could find any clues to his whereabouts. She'd noted the house had two large trees in the yard, and there was a dark alley running behind the place. She had a plan.

Magda Nowak, Bryan Mitchell's most-of-the-time girlfriend, was nobody's fool. She had been one of the first females to graduate from the U.S. Army Ranger school and had been deployed overseas twice before leaving the military two years ago. After returning to her hometown of Spokane, she'd reunited with Bryan, whom she'd dated in high school, and accepted his offer to work for him as a security officer until she figured out what her next step would be. She hadn't quite made up her mind what her next chapter in life might be because she was currently focused on something else: Money.

Like all the employees at Preston, she knew about the two-million-dollar reward for anyone who could capture or kill Xana. Her thoughts about the reward were very simple—she wanted it all for herself. She viewed Preston Security as a useful asset for gathering intel, but ultimately she intended to be the one to claim the reward, confident in her superior intellect, skills, and capacity for violence.

Initially, Magda had considered sharing the reward with Bryan. However, when she caught him cheating on her with a call girl that thought went straight out the window. It had taken all her discipline to act like she'd reconciled with him when, in actuality, she was just using him to get the two million for herself. If she had to kill Bryan or others to make that happen, so be it. She comforted herself by viewing her scheme as a mission, a mission that demanded she be fake with Bryan, at least for the time being.

Magda had spent a lot of time thinking about Xana and learned as many details of her life and actions as she could. She had some admiration for the woman because she could tell Xana had brains, guts, loyalty, surprising abilities, and could certainly hold a grudge. It was almost like she'd been to Ranger school or something, and Magda cautioned herself to be careful. No amount of money was worth dying for, but two million was enough to take some reasonable risks.

It was frustrating to her when some of Bryan's dealers were arrested, and Bryan was forced into hiding. It meant her intel-gathering machine had been diminished, and that she needed to pick up the slack on her own. She tried to put herself in Xana's shoes to predict what Xana would do when she learned of the death of the ex-cop and of the attempt on the other ex-cop's life. She realized she had only to envision what she would do in that situation—she would try to visit violence upon the heads of those involved. And the logical place to start would be with Bryan and his house. After some consideration, she had Bryan contact the alarm company that monitored his home system to arrange for them to forward alarm notifications only to her phone. Her reasoning, as she explained to Bryan, was that they didn't want the police around his house and that she would respond to any alarms. This served two purposes for Magda: First, she could be in or near the residence in case Xana went there. Secondly, it allowed her an excuse to be away from Bryan, who she didn't really feel like being around anyway.

Xana waited a couple days for the moon to diminish, then prepared to enter Bryan's residence. She put on a dark blonde wig with a black stocking cap and dark, warm clothing. At about three A.M. she arrived in Bryan's neighborhood, parked her rental van in the parking lot of a small tavern, locked the vehicle, and slowly walked to the alley behind his house in the slushy snow. She was wearing waterproof hiking shoes, but some snow managed to get to her socks and her ankles felt wet and cold. When she was adjacent to his house, she climbed a four-foot fence and walked up to one of the trees. There, she waited and listened for a few minutes—there was a dog barking in the distance but nothing else. Xana knew that second-story windows weren't always alarmed and was hoping that was the case with Bryan's house. Looking up into the tree she was next to, she chose a sturdy branch and began her ascent. When she reached the second-floor roof, she saw there was a two-foot gap she needed to jump across—the tree was swaying a little and the jump was going to be more difficult than she was expecting. Coiling herself on a thick branch, she gritted her teeth and sprang across the gap. She landed on the roof on all fours, with just a little noise. There was some snow on the bottom edge of the roof that her right foot began to slide on, but she was able to transfer her weight to her hands and crawled up the roof a few feet to the first window. It was cold and breezy as she reached inside her coat for her cell phone. Using the dim light from her phone's screen, she carefully inspected the window. She didn't see any obvious alarm sensors, and noted the window had an old-fashioned, wooden frame that swung outward, with a brass latch that was currently locking it in place. She put her phone away and removed a small pry bar from another interior pocket. The pry bar was warm from her body but quickly grew cold as she began prying next to the latch. It was difficult, but eventually the screws on half of the latch began to pull loose, and finally the window could be swung open. Xana crawled inside the room, remained for a few seconds, then crawled back out the window and returned to the tree. Once she was on the ground, she made it back across the backyard fence and watched the property from a half-block away for about twenty minutes, to make sure there was no response to a possible alarm. The time passed very slowly, but eventually the twenty minutes was up and she began moving again. She moved back to the property, up the tree, and back into the room. Inside, she paused to pull on a pair of medical gloves and looked around. The room appeared to be a little-used bedroom that didn't contain much except a twin-sized bed. Xana wanted to find a home office where she could look through records and perhaps find a hint of Bryan's current location. Walking to the interior door, she opened it slowly and slid into the hallway. Everything was dark and she couldn't hear or smell anything unusual. There were two more bedrooms upstairs, one of which appeared to be the master bedroom. Next to it, she found what she was looking for: A room which contained a large desk, a long credenza, and two file cabinets.

She closed the door and window shades to the room, put on a hiker's rechargeable headlamp, and began quickly perusing the files. Most were of no use to her, but eventually she found a folder that contained several utility bills. There were two bills for power and internet which listed an address she did not recognize—she quickly photographed them with her phone. Nothing else in the room appeared to be of any importance to her, and she put everything back in place as she prepared to leave.

As she opened the door to go back into the hallway, she was stunned to see a powerful looking woman standing in the hallway. The woman immediately kicked her hard in the sternum with the bottom of her foot and Xana flew backwards into the room; she was only saved from injury by executing a ninja-style back roll as she hit the ground. She was instantly back on her feet and she and the woman began circling each other in an open space next to the desk. The woman jumped in and grabbed for her hair, a move which Xana countered by punching her sharply in the throat. The woman moved back, clutching the wig and hat Xana had been wearing: She threw them aside and came at Xana with a quick right hook. Xana was only able to partially block the punch and fell to the ground as she felt a solid impact on her left ear. As the woman rushed up to her, Xana was able to draw one leg back and deliver a powerful kick between the woman's legs—her opponent howled in pain and fell on top of her. The close proximity triggered an intense hand battle which ended when they each had a death grip on the other's hair. They lay on the ground, facing each other, breathing heavily.

"You kicked me where I live, wig-bitch," snarled the woman.

"Great, now I have to burn that shoe." The woman was clearly much stronger than her and Xana would have to rely on technique and dirty tricks to win the fight. She had her Sig P-365 on her, but didn't want to use it unless there was no other choice;

she knew the neighbors would instantly call 911 if they heard a gunshot. The woman pinned Xana's head to the ground and began to lift her head out of Xana's grip, ripping out her own hair in the process. Xana knew she was going to lose a pure strength battle and twisted one of her hands so she could dig her left thumbnail into the woman's right eye, trying to gouge it out. The woman howled in pain again and let go of Xana's hair, clutching her own face instead. Xana jumped to her feet, kicked the woman in the head until she lost consciousness, and stood there on shaky legs for a moment. She spotted her wig, hat, and tattered medical gloves on the floor and stuffed them in her coat pockets; she then patted the woman down, looking for identification. The only helpful item she found was a military dog tag on a chain around the woman's neck which she took a photo of, then she climbed out the window and back down the tree. When she reached the alley, she started a slow, quiet run back to her minivan. While driving back to her hotel, she replayed the incident in her mind. Who was this Magda Nowak?

Magda woke up with a sore head, an aching jaw and throat, bruised genitals, and an eye that really hurt. She rolled onto her belly, brought her knees up, and struggled to a kneeling position. Nausea hit her hard, and she reached out a hand to the desk to steady herself until it subsided—then she slowly stood up and staggered to the second-floor bathroom. In the light of the vanity, she checked herself out. There were swelling red marks on the left side of her face and scalp, her hair was falling out in clumps, and her right eye was a bloody mess. She pulled her eyelids open for a closer look at the eye: It looked like the bloody spot was in the white part of her inner eye, and the pupil area looked intact. There didn't appear to be any ocular fluid leaking from the injury. Still, she knew the eye, and her other injuries, would take a while to recover from.

She was enormously disappointed in herself, because she'd been so sure she could overpower Xana before deciding what to do with her. Her plan to catch Xana in the house had worked perfectly, and she'd had the element of surprise as she confronted Xana in the second-floor office. She'd nailed Xana with her best front kick to the chest, only to see her come up off the ground like a fucking pop-tart. In the flurry that followed, somehow the little bitch had kicked her in the genitals so hard she'd almost vomited, matched her as they each went for a hair hold, then nearly put her eye out. Then the ass-kicking, in the form of head-kicking, had really started and she'd been knocked out. Now, instead of being two million dollars richer, she could only limp around with a damaged self-image.

It was not a good day.

CHAPTER 12

Xana sat in her hotel room, using her laptop to find out what she could about Magda. Apparently, she'd been a star volleyball player in high school, as there were a few older news articles about her leading a Spokane-area high school team to a state championship. There were numerous articles a couple years later praising Magda for being one of the first female graduates of the U.S. Army Ranger school. Xana knew that was a solid accomplishment, and she guessed the woman went on to have an exceptional military career. But how had Magda gone from being a star to hiding out in a drug dealer's house, trying to get a reward from the cartel? There were no obvious answers. Xana was aware the cartel had promised a reward to anyone who could capture or kill her—she wasn't sure of the amount but guessed it must be substantial if it could lure people like Magda into breaking the law.

Xana knew she'd been fortunate to escape injury during the encounter she'd had. In her mind, she thanked her now-dead uncle who had enrolled her in Ninjutsu classes so many years ago when she was just a teenager. The ground-rolling and the mentality of fighting with no rules except to survive had served her well, but Xana held no illusions: She knew that any physical confrontation carried enormous risks, and that there was no guarantee whatsoever she would prevail if the two were to go at it again. She knew she needed to be very careful.

Opening her phone, she pulled up the photos of the utility bills she'd taken at Bryan's office. They were both for a residence with a Newport, Washington address—she didn't know where that was but opened a map program and saw that it was a small town about fifty miles north and a little east of Spokane. The address was for a small house in a wooded area a little to the west of the town, and it looked like a good place to hide. She found a couple places on the map where she might park her 4Runner a little to the north of the house and decided to do some snooping around the area that evening.

By six P.M., Xana was dressed in warm outdoor clothing and was driving towards Newport. She arrived at the location where she'd noted the possible parking areas—the first had plowed snow mounded up on it and was not usable, but the second appeared to be a spot where snowmobilers loaded and unloaded their machines. It was vacant, and she found a place to park that was out of sight from the road. After checking and double-checking her gear, she locked her 4Runner and began walking toward the house in the dark. It was a windless, dark night, and the tall trees and snow gave her an uncomfortable flashback of her escape from Preston Security. For most of the way, she was able to follow a snowmobile trail but had to walk through trees and snow for the last hundred yards. When she could see the back of the house, she paused for a few minutes but, after seeing no activity, moved again to where she could see the side and front of the place. The porch light was on, but all the shades were closed and she saw no activity inside. After an hour, the lack of movement caused her to feel chilled but she told herself to give it another hour or two. After about forty-five minutes, an older Nissan pulled up to the house and an attractive woman in her early thirties got out of the vehicle. Despite the cold temperature, the woman was wearing a light denim jacket, open at the front, and a cut-off shirt that showed a lot of skin. The woman struck a sexy pose as she rang the doorbell, and Xana thought she knew what was going on—she believed the woman to be a call girl. The door opened and the woman walked right in, as if she'd been there before. An idea was forming in Xana's head, and she silently walked back to her vehicle, started it, and drove to the road the house was on. She passed the house, noted that the Nissan was still there, and travelled down the road about a half mile in the direction the woman had come from. After finding a place to watch the road, she turned off her lights and checked her phone for the time. If her suspicions were correct, she figured the woman would be driving by within an hour or so. As expected, she eventually saw the Nissan driving past her location—she let it get a distance down the road, then pulled out to follow. Most people, Xana knew, paid no attention to the vehicles behind them, especially at night when all they could see were the headlights of those to the rear. Still, she varied the distance she was trailing behind the Nissan and changed lanes a couple times to present some variety. She followed the woman all the way to east Spokane, where she saw the Nissan pull into a parking lot of a strip club. A sign in front of the building indicated the unimaginative name of the place to be "Desires". Xana parked next to the woman, rolled down her passenger window, and spoke to her as the woman exited her car.

"Hello, can I get a little of your time? I'll make it worth your while." The woman looked around the parking lot, then looked at Xana.

"Well, I normally don't date women, but for you I might make an exception. You're way hot." She warily opened the passenger door, sat down next to Xana, and closed the door. "What do you have in mind?"

"Nothing physical, I just want to talk to you, maybe get some advice." She handed the woman a few hundred-dollar bills. "What's your name?"

The woman took the money. "Around here I go by Chloe, but you're paying, so you can call me whatever you want."

"I'll go with Chloe, thank you. I'll be up front with you and let you know that I'm not a cop, and I'm not trying to get you in any trouble. I do have some questions though, about the man you were just with—I saw your car at his place about an hour ago."

The woman looked surprised. "Am I that easy to follow? I guess I am, or you wouldn't be here." She shook her head. "You must mean Bryan, then. He's not my favorite client, but he's been pretty reliable for the past few months. If he's in trouble or goes away for some reason, I'm out a lot of money. I'm going to pass on the questions." She handed the money back and started to get out of the car.

"I may have an opportunity for you that would get you more money than you'd ever get from Bryan. But first I need to ask the questions."

Chloe hesitated, looking at the money. After a minute, she took the cash again. "What is the opportunity?"

"I'll explain in a minute. But first, why do you say he's not your favorite client?"

"A few reasons. First, he's a huge dude, very intense and scary. He always has guns around. His girlfriend is scary as well, an ex-Army type who already caught me with Bryan once. She's probably going to stomp my ass if she catches me again. And when I'm there and we get down to business, he always wants to use meth first and he's really rough. The only reason I keep going back is because he tips me better than anyone else."

"Do you know his girlfriend's name?"

"Yeah, it's Magda."

"Okay. Well, Chloe, I'll just tell you that Bryan may have hurt a friend of mine, and I'm trying to figure out as much about him as I can. So first, why is he even up here and not in Spokane where his business is? And I mean his drug business as well as his security business."

"Right. He says it's because the cops are after him, and I believe it. He's cut his beard off, trimmed his hair, and hardly ever goes anywhere. He hasn't gone into any details, but he probably killed someone or got caught up in a drug bust."

"All right. Who does he get his drugs from?"

"Well, now you're making me nervous, and I don't want to talk too much about that. I'll just say that they're these guys that come up from Mexico...I've dated a couple of them, and they're even scarier than Bryan."

"I won't ask anything else about them, for now. But who is running things down in Spokane if Bryan just stays up here?"

"I hear Bryan on the phone all the time with his dealers. It sounds like Magda is running the security jobs, but there aren't many of them anymore."

"Why do you and Bryan carry on at the house if you're so scared of her?"

"He says he can figure out when she won't be around. But trust me, it's on my mind every second I'm there."

Xana thought for a moment. "Here's the opportunity, Chloe. The next time he wants you to go over, I want to go in your place.

Tell him you are sick, whatever, and that you've worked with me before. You'll just have to sell it. If you can make that happen, I'll give you fifty grand as soon as he agrees. But here's a warning—you should be prepared to move out of the area as soon as I give you the money. I hear there's a lot of clubs in Portland, maybe you could move there and start over. And don't ask or worry about my plans with him. The less you know, the safer you'll be."

"Are you insane? I mean, I don't know what your plans are, but he's at least twice your size!"

"I'm only insane when I have to be, but you won't have to worry about that. Are you in, or am I wasting my time?"

"I'm in. It's time for me to get out of this place, anyway. How are we going to do this when he calls me?"

"The next time he calls, tell him you'll call back in a couple of hours, that's how much time I'll need to get myself ready and meet you back here in the parking lot. I'll want to listen in on the call when you talk to him, so be thinking about what you'll say. When he agrees, I'll give you the cash and you'll be out."

"Most girls couldn't do what you are going to try. But you have the aura and the looks, so damned if I don't think you can do it."

If she only knew, thought Xana to herself. "One last thing before I leave—I need to get the phone number Bryan's been using to contact you."

Once she provided the number, Chloe got out of the car and Xana began the drive back to her hotel, thinking about how she needed to alter her appearance for when she met Bryan. He'd seen a photo of her, so she needed to be careful. She already had a blonde wig she could use, but she needed some better makeup and an outfit that would distract him. She'd seen a large shopping mall in Spokane Valley, just east of Spokane proper, and figured she could find what she needed there.

By the end of the next day, she had everything she needed, including a small knife she could hide in the voluminous wig she'd be wearing. In her hotel room, she experimented with her new makeup, arrived at a style she thought would work, then put on her complete outfit. When she'd left the cartel, she had hoped her days of dressing in such a manner were behind her. It gave her a sad feeling to look at herself in the mirror, so she took everything off, took a shower, and climbed into bed.

It went against her nature to have to wait for something, but she knew she was stuck until the call from Chloe came in. Three days passed, then four. She couldn't stop thinking about Jake, about how he'd dropped everything to get her off the mountain when she was freezing to death, and how he'd been shot while trying to protect her in the airport parking lot...and how, horrifically, he'd been killed. She thought about how she'd been with him while she was helping him recuperate at his house—she hadn't been a bitch with him, really, but neither had she been as caring and loving as she now wished she'd been. Instead, she'd been lukewarm and distant, thinking she was saving his feelings. He'd made sure she knew the intensity of his feelings when he kissed her goodbye on the day she left, and she had reciprocated. Oh yeah, had she reciprocated. She hadn't felt like that for a man before, and what had she done about it? She'd run away.

Xana wondered, as she often had since she was a child, if she was just destined to have a miserable life, full of trauma, violence, and upsetting circumstances. So many people, it seemed to her, were living lives that were fortunate indeed. She thought of the happy mothers she'd seen at the mall just the other day, pushing strollers around, talking on their cell phones, smiling and laughing. While they were buying maternity clothing, she'd been buying an assassin's disguise. Instead of talking about what funny things a two-year-old had said, she was considering which shape of knife blade was best for cutting a man's throat. It all made her question why she even existed. She got up, walked to the hotel room mirror, and looked herself in the eyes. The reflection didn't provide much information concerning the question she had. She looked again at her reflection, deeper, trying desperately to see something, anything. Who are you, she was asking. She received no response.

On the eighth day, Chloe called just as it was getting dark. Xana quickly put on her makeup, outfit, and wig. She'd already concealed her knife in the back of her wig, by sewing it in place with some light thread. When she was ready, she put her Sig P365 and fifty thousand dollars in cash into her purse, got into her rented minivan, and drove to the strip club parking lot. Chloe was already there and climbed into the passenger seat of the minivan, looking Xana over as she did so.

"Holy Hell! Girl, I'm glad you're not my actual competition, I'd never get any work."

"Do I look differently than how I did when you saw me last week?"

"Definitely. And everything goes together perfectly." She looked at Xana out of the side of her eye. "It's almost as if you've done this kind of thing before."

Xana let the comment slide. "I see. So, how did it go when Bryan called you?"

"I think it was fine, I just told him I had the flu, with vomiting and diarrhea. That turned him off. But then I told him about you, and said you were new but that I'd worked with you a couple times already. And, of course, that you are the hottest thing around, which is true. He's interested and asked me your name. I had no idea what name you wanted to use, so I just said it was Destiny, which was the first thing that came to mind. I know it's dumb, but we all go by dumb names, sorry. I told him I'd call back to confirm, which I should do pretty quickly—that is, if our deal is still on."

"It's still on. Go ahead and make the call, but keep the phone by your left ear; I'm going to put my head right next to yours so I can hear what he's saying."

Chloe made the call, and Xana thought she did a good job of selling the situation. When it was over, Bryan was expecting the new girl to arrive at his Newport house in a little over an hour. Xana handed over a rubber-banded packet of hundred-dollar bills to Chloe and told her to be careful.

"Thank you, I'm taking your advice and getting out of town right away. You be careful too, whatever it is that you're doing."

"Will do." Chloe left the minivan and was gone. Xana began the northbound drive out of Spokane, gathering her thoughts about what was to come. Unless things went very wrong, Bryan was not going to see another sunrise. However, she wanted to question him before she killed him, to find out more about who had killed Jake and tried to kill Doc. She knew this mission would require all of her skills and courage to complete, but she was filled with resolve. As she drove, she concentrated on her breathing and envisioned herself giving Bryan a fake smile as he opened the door for her. She could tell it was windy outside, much in contrast to her first visit to the house. At least it wasn't snowing, she thought, but cursed a few minutes later when she began to see a few snowflakes in her headlights. A little snow wouldn't be a problem, but the last thing she wanted was to be involved in an accident after leaving Bryan dead. She continued on, and the snow increased slightly the farther from Spokane she travelled. When she got close to her destination, she reminded herself again to breathe evenly and to be prepared for surprises. As she pulled up to the house, she carefully backed up near the front door so she could make a rapid escape if she had to. Then she turned off her vehicle, checked her makeup quickly in the rear-view mirror, grabbed her purse, and walked up to the door. Bryan opened the door before she had a chance to ring the doorbell, and she gave him a slow, sultry smile.

"You must be the lovely Destiny, come on in."

"Thank you. I'm happy to meet you, Bryan." She gave him a quick hug, thinking it was like hugging one of the giant trees outside. Chloe hadn't been lying about his size. They sat down on the couch and made a little small talk before they started talking about business. Bryan eventually gave her some cash, and said he would tip her after their session. The next part was crucial to Xana's plan.

"Listen, why don't you sit down in a chair and let me rub your shoulders for a bit. It will give us both a chance to warm up on such a cold night."

"I like the way you think," he said, and sat down in one of the living room chairs. She moved behind him and started rubbing his shoulders and neck with both hands, and then after a minute reached up with her right hand and tugged loose the knife she had concealed in her wig. She put the blade up against his throat and pulled back so that it was on the verge of cutting him. He gasped and moved his head back as far as he could, but she kept the pressure on the knife.

"The fun part is over. Allow me to introduce myself: My name is Xana. I think you've heard of me before. I'm going to ask you some questions which you are going to answer. The reason you are going to answer is because if you don't, I'm going to cut your throat wide open."

"You bitch; I'm really looking forward to ripping your fucking head off!"

"Well, I'm pretty sure I'm going to be the only one with a memory of our brief and unhappy relationship. Your only chance of not seeing your own blood in a few seconds is to answer my questions."

Bryan was able to maintain his bluster for a couple more minutes, but then the reality of his chance of dying set in and he began to answer her questions: He told Xana his abilities and freedom of movement had been reduced after he was almost arrested, so he'd called his connection at the cartel for help. The cartel had put him in touch with a sniper who went by the name Zeke to take care of Jake, and had assigned a couple other operatives to take care of the physician. He showed Xana the numbers he had on his phone for Zeke and for his cartel connection.

Before she could finish her interrogation, the front door suddenly flew open and Magda rushed in, a furious expression on her face. Her expression turned to surprise as she looked hard at Xana, recognizing her, then quickly turned back to fury as she charged across the living room. Xana ripped the knife across Bryan's throat and turned to face Magda, planting one foot well behind herself to counter the force she knew was coming. Concealing the knife behind her leg, she waited until Magda was almost upon her then lifted it to the level of Magda's neck. Magda's motion carried her forward and she impaled herself upon the blade, her eyes growing wide with shock and pain. Xana cut to the left with the knife and then stood aside as Magda fell next to Bryan, both bleeding profusely, gasping, and gurgling.

Xana grabbed Bryan's phone and wiped the blood from it with a kitchen towel so she could record the numbers he'd been showing her. By the time she was finished, both Bryan and Magda were dead. She found another towel and wiped down the phone again, as well as the interior surfaces she had touched. When she walked out the front door, she saw that Magda's still-running vehicle was blocking her minivan. Entering Magda's vehicle, she re-parked it, turned the ignition off, and took the keys inside. She used the towel again to wipe down the keys as well as Magda's vehicle handle and interior, then went back inside. Once she made a final check to make sure she'd left nothing behind, she used the towel to lock and shut the front door and left the house in her minivan.

She was trembling a little as she drove back to Spokane. Things certainly hadn't gone as she expected, but she wasn't sorry that Bryan was dead. She wasn't quite sure how she felt about Magda, but decided she was safer in a world that didn't include the woman. When she reached her hotel, she checked herself for blood. There were a few splashes on her shirt, but she was able to put on a jacket to cover them as she walked to her room. Inside, she removed her outfit, put it in a bag along with her wig and makeup, then took a shower. When she was clean and had dried her hair she got back in her minivan with the bag, drove to Spokane Valley, and dropped the bag in a grocery store garbage can.

Back in her room she went to bed and slept fitfully until morning. At around ten A.M. she had a call from Nina, who let her know she would have to return to Phoenix for another possible court hearing.

CHAPTER 13

Zeke was in Las Vegas, spending some of his earnings from the Jake Connor hit, when he received a call from the cartel. Bryan Mitchell, with whom Zeke had worked with in the past, was not responding to calls and Zeke was directed to immediately proceed to the residence near Newport, Washington to see what was going on.

It was early evening when Zeke took the call. He took a nap, then began the long drive north in his Camry—in was late the following day when he arrived in Spokane. While refueling his vehicle, an idea struck him and he filled a five-gallon gas can from his trunk as well. He slept for a while in a hotel room and then made the drive up to the Newport house, arriving at about two-thirty A.M. There was absolutely no one out and about on the roads and Zeke didn't feel like parking a distance away and tromping through the frozen woods. Instead, he decided to forego some of his usual caution and parked right in front of the place. There was already another car parked out front, and before approaching the house on foot he pulled open the garage door and saw a huge white truck that looked like something Bryan would drive. Alongside the house he observed another, smaller white pickup truck. Zeke knocked on the door and tried to look through the living room window—no one answered but he thought he saw someone's legs on the floor. After splintering the jamb with a sharp kick, he entered the house and saw Bryan, dead on the floor with a sliced neck. Next to Bryan was a powerful-looking female, also dead and with a neck injury, who Zeke assumed was Bryan's girlfriend Magda. On the kitchen counter, Zeke spotted a phone—it was locked, but he used Bryan's thumb to unlock it. Bryan's torso was beginning to bloat and smell, but his fingers were only slightly shriveled. He checked the recent activity and saw many unanswered calls and texts from the past day or two. Prior to that, he noted several calls and texts from Magda and from someone named Chloe. Zeke didn't know anything about anyone named Chloe, but he wondered if "Chloe" was actually Xana, and he made a note of the number. There was no way to tell and no one to ask, but the dead bodies seemed to speak for themselves. He felt a chill as he looked at the bodies and wondered: If this had been Xana's work, how had she managed to kill two people who were obviously stronger than her? After taking photos of the calls and texts, he rummaged around the house a little. A little extra cash never hurt anyone, and he found a few thousand dollars in various denominations which he stuffed in his pants pocket. Looking further, he found a couple AR-15 rifles and a HK USP .45. He took the firearms out to his Camry and stuffed them under a blanket in his trunk, then grabbed the five-gallon gas can and began dumping gas all over the interior of the house. When the can was empty, he put it back in the trunk and closed the trunk lid. Standing in the doorway, he held a small lighter to a pool of gasoline and watched as the blaze quickly spread. He left the front door open to fuel the fire, got into his Camry, and left. After driving east through the small town of Newport, he crossed into Idaho and drove south on Hwy 41 until he reached I-90. From there, he drove to his hotel, reported his findings to the cartel, and caught up on his sleep.

The next morning, Zeke picked up the clothing he'd worn the night before and held them up to his nose—sure enough, they smelled like death. He washed them in the hotel laundry room a couple times and dried them with a scented fabric softener sheet. Back in his room, he watched the local news for a while but there were no reports about the fire. Turning off the television, he sat in a corner chair and thought, as he often did, about the two-million-dollar reward for Xana. His competitors for the reward at Preston Security were dwindling by the second, it seemed, and he felt reinvigorated by his improved chances. After thinking for several minutes, he called the cartel and asked that an attempt be made to determine the location of the phone used by Chloe. Cell phone employees with access to such information were sought after by the cartel and there were several who were on the payroll. That afternoon, he was provided with an address in downtown Portland that the phone was at most of the time—the address, he was told, was a small extended-stay hotel and the phone was normally in a unit at the north end of the place.

By late afternoon the following day, Zeke was also a guest at the extended-stay hotel, which was located in a rather seedy area of downtown Portland. He wanted to finish his business there quickly before his Camry was broken into and had made sure that Chloe's room was visible from the front windows of his room. At around seven P.M., he observed a young woman exit the room and made note of which vehicle she got into as she left. It was definitely not Xana, he saw to his disappointment. Three hours later he spotted the same car pulling back into the parking lot, and he left his room so he would arrive at the woman's door as she did. As she was opening her door, Zeke approached her and held out his phone— he asked her if the phone was hers; when she involuntarily looked at it he punched her hard on the side of her jaw. He dragged the stunned woman inside her room and closed the door.

When Chloe had begun to recover, Zeke displayed a small knife and began to question her about her phone number being on Bryan's phone. With a quavering voice, she answered his questions truthfully. When she'd finished explaining it all, he asked her to show her the name in her contacts associated with the phone the mystery woman had used—she showed him how she had used the name "Pretty" because she had no idea what the woman's true name had been. Zeke made a note of the number and then, with a sad feeling inside, made Chloe tell him where she'd hidden the fifty thousand dollars. After she told him, he gripped her hair in one hand and her jaw in the other, preparing to snap her neck. However, he looked down at her face, and she looked so scared and pitiful that he couldn't do it. He didn't think he'd ever be able to look his mother in the eye again if he did it. As he let go of her, he looked down and saw her small hands still gripping his arms. He disengaged from them but seemed to feel a chill where they had been and, after brushing his arms with his hands, the chill persisted. He turned from her and told her to keep the money. Then he left her room, gathered his belongings from his own room, and headed out of town. It was late and he was tired, but he couldn't leave Portland quickly enough; the city and his actions there had given him a deep depression. He drove all the way to Baker City and checked into a room. Before going to bed, he called the cartel and asked them to locate the phone he was sure belonged to Xana. In the morning, he was notified of the results: All information pertaining to the phone had been locked, pursuant to a court order obtained by Captain Nina Vasquez of the Arizona Department of Public Safety.

CHAPTER 14

Nina had a feeling of unease as she looked around the courtroom contained within the federal courthouse in Phoenix. The room was packed with defendants, attorneys, family members, and members of the press. She and the senior Assistant U.S. Attorney sat at the prosecutor's table in front of the imposing judge's bench, effectively surrounded by criminals of the worst kind. Thankfully, because the case involved the cartel, there was also a massive presence from the U.S. Marshal's service as well as from members of the AZDPS. A Phoenix PD SWAT team was in reserve on the top floor of the courthouse, in case anything went seriously amiss. Still, Nina knew that a lot of damage could be done in a short period of time and cautioned herself to keep her wits about her.

On tap was a hearing to suppress the evidence from the wiretap case which had resulted in the arrests of the cartel members and their associates. If the evidence from the wire could not be used almost all of the criminal charges would be dismissed, so the defense attorneys had been planning and developing a strategy for months to get the wire overturned. It was a long shot. Nina and her federal partners had put together a solid case and it would, they felt, take a minor miracle for the defense to win the hearing.

The miracle the defense had been banking on for months was that Xana, a key witness for the prosecution, would become unavailable to testify. The defense attorneys, as officers of the court, had to act like they didn't know their clients were trying to kill Xana. However, they all found the money from the cartel to be irresistible and they certainly were not above becoming errand boys and girls for their clients: They were quite willing to pass written notes from the defendants to family members, for instance, or to pass along short phone messages to cartel associates who were not locked up. It was all fair game, they deluded themselves into thinking, while marveling at the velocity with which their bank accounts were growing.

When it became apparent that Xana was ready and willing to testify at the hearing, the defense attorneys made a collective push to have the hearing continued once again. However, the judge had come to terms with the fact that he would have to preside over the giant case and now just wanted to get it over with. He announced that the hearing would go on as scheduled and, on a blustery Tuesday morning, the hearing began. The entire morning session was taken up as various defense attorneys began popping up one by one, anxious for their clients to see them vigorously presenting arguments about why their client's charges should be dropped. All requests for dismissal were denied. By late morning, the judge was weary of the shenanigans and decreed that the hearing would begin in earnest after lunch.

During the lunch hour Nina met with Xana, who had been stashed inside a guarded room within the U.S. Attorney's office section of the courthouse. She noted earlier that Xana was professionally dressed and looked like an attorney herself.

"How are you doing, Xana?"

"I'm fine, I'm just anxious to get this over with. What's going on in the courtroom?"

"A lot of theater so far, the defense attorneys are making individual bogus requests for dismissal. The judge isn't having any more of it and wants to get started after lunch. The defense attorneys have chosen one person to make an opening argument for them all, and of course the AUSA will have an opening argument as well. Then it will be time for testimony, and the judge has agreed to let you testify first, to limit your exposure as much as possible. I'll be testifying eventually, as will a few federal agents who worked on the case...the hearing will probably last about three days, but if all goes well you'll be done today."

"And assuming our side wins, what happens next?"

"Well, hopefully the judge makes a decision right away, but he may not. Sometimes it can take weeks to get a ruling. But usually, once the prosecution wins the motion to suppress a wiretap the negotiations for guilty pleas begin in earnest."

"Ok, and the questions the attorneys can ask me—they are only supposed to be about things that led up to the wiretap case, correct?"

Nina was picking up on a little edge to Xana's voice. "Yes—the AUSA will be on the lookout for them trying to go too far afield, and she'll jump in if necessary. But remember, you are seen as a victim in the overall case, so don't worry. Just tell the truth and nothing but the truth. Like we talked about before, they may try and get under your skin to elicit some type of emotional reaction from you. Don't fall for that, but you don't need to let them bully you either. Just tell the truth and be yourself."

"All right. I'm good at being calm. Well, at appearing to be calm anyway. I'll do my best."

It wasn't until mid-afternoon that Xana took the stand. The judge told everyone to buckle in for a long day, because they were all going to stay in court until Xana was excused. Nina watched with a little apprehension as the first defense attorney asked Xana a few innocuous opening questions. His next questions weren't so innocuous.

"So," he was saying. "You are an ex-prostitute, is that correct?"

"No. Nothing could be further from the truth."

"Well, what do you say is the truth?"

"The truth is I was enslaved by your client and the others here and forced to do things of a sexual nature against my will. If I hadn't done them I, along with my aunt and uncle, would have been killed."

"But you received many things of value, isn't that correct? A condominium, a car, beautiful clothing, cash, all expenses paid. It really sounds like the life of a prostitute to me, doesn't it to you?"

Xana's face was calm, but her eyes were not. "Sir, I would have chosen to live my life barefoot in a hut rather than to have gone through what I did. And I'd go to that hut right now if it would divest me of the memories I carry. The things you describe were props, nothing more."

Nina watched as one defense attorney after another tried to ruffle Xana without success. She noted that none of them wanted to delve too much into the facts of what their clients had done before the wiretap; rather they sought to dehumanize her and to make her seem like an emotional creature of low intellect—a person who may not be a good factual witness. It was not working. The AUSA's questions, by contrast, were all about the facts of what the defendants had done. She used skillful questions to guide Xana into telling her story, beginning with how she had been kidnapped into the cartel at the age of eighteen. Xana went on to describe how she had been able to escape her kidnapper and rapist, but how her life was not much improved as she was immediately sent to the U.S. to seduce men from whom the cartel wished to extract information. She finished by describing how her life had changed once she met Nina and how she, at great risk to herself, had cooperated with authorities to help bring down the cartel.

At the end of the long day, a couple of the defense attorneys tried to ask Xana about murders and thefts which had taken place after the initiation of the wiretap. The questions were objected to by the AUSA as not being pertinent to the hearing, and the judge did not require Xana to answer. The long day in court was finally over.

Nina put into motion a plan she'd developed to get Xana safely out of the courthouse and back to the AZDPS training center where they were staying during the hearing. When they arrived, Nina sat with Xana as they had some food in the cafeteria.

"I'm really proud of you, Xana, those attorneys didn't lay a finger on you. And you were so poised, even while sitting there amongst all those cartel members! I'm seriously impressed."

"Well, I had a little trick up my sleeve—I just imagined I was Nina Vasquez up there taking all those questions. It really helped me keep my cool. I was pretty nervous at the beginning, but then it was like being in a fight, and once I'd taken a couple hits I calmed down and went to work, so to speak."

"Whatever the technique, the results can't be argued with. The AUSA wanted me to pass along her compliments for how you handled yourself up there, by the way."

"That's nice to hear. So, what happens next?"

"The hearing is going to go on for a couple more days, and then we'll see how quickly the judge makes a decision. I'm stuck there; in fact I'll be the one testifying tomorrow. I think you should just hang out here until it's over, so we'll both know what the situation is. Are you OK with that?"

"Sure, I kind of like it here; it's nice to feel safe. As long as there's food and a gym I'm happy."

"I'm glad you feel that way. I've been here so much over the past year or so that it grates on me a little bit, but I predict I'll survive. It's getting late, are you ready to call it a night?"

"Definitely, my eyes are getting heavy."

"I'll see you in the morning."

Nina spent the next two days in court as the hearing inched its way along. Like Xana, she testified for several hours and had to run a verbal gauntlet of attorneys trying to attack the case in various ways. She felt prepared and simply testified to the truth, as simply and concisely as she could. Finally it was over, ending as the judge announced he'd have a decision the following morning.

That night, she and Xana discussed the hearing and the court processes that would follow. After, Xana was silent for a couple minutes and Nina asked her what was on her mind.

"Oh, I've just been having some inner struggles. You know, while I was with the cartel I had no freedom, so my actions were dictated by the people who were controlling me. Once I got away, I was busy trying to stay alive and roaming all over creation. Now that this hearing is almost over, and will hopefully lead to these guys pleading guilty, I'm trying to fathom my next step. It's really difficult because I can't even answer basic questions about myself—such as, who am I, and why do I even exist? I've done some bad things, and not all of them were forced upon me. Does that make me a horrible person? I feel like I'm trying to make decisions without a foundation. And the worst thing is that my brain always, by default it seems, assumes I'm just destined to have an existence full of pain and death. And, that I pass the pain and death on to others—look what happened to poor Jake, for instance. Sometimes I just want to crawl into a hole and never come out."

"Those are all tough questions," said Nina. "But the fact that you are asking them, it seems to me, is a good sign: It means you are moving past survival mode and beginning to live life on your own terms. Maybe it will help, as you go forward, to think about responding to those questions as a journey, one in which you are free to think whatever you wish. And there's no time limit, hell, who among us really has all the answers? Not me, nor anyone I know."

"Somehow you always say things that make me feel better. Thank you."

"Remember, I've seen you in the clinch, when the true colors show. Some people's true colors are ugly. Not yours. Your true colors shine like gold, Xana. They shine like gold. And that's how I know you are going to be okay."

The next morning, the courtroom was packed again as everyone gathered to hear the judge's ruling. The defense attorneys chatted amiably among themselves, while the defendants looked anxious and uneasy. Nina and the AUSA sat stoically at their table: They expected to win the hearing, but they also knew that judges often made the wrong call and so prepared themselves for bad news. One of the court clerks had mentioned to them that the judge had been in his chambers since five o'clock that morning. There was little sense in trying to guess what that meant; they figured he was simply trying to get his facts straight one way or the other.

Finally, at a little after nine o'clock, the judge entered the courtroom. After a few preliminary matters he began to announce his decision—a long-winded one it was, as he went through the various arguments the defense attorneys had presented and began to shoot them down, one by one. Nina started to have a good feeling about the outcome of the hearing and was relieved when he finally gave his ruling that the evidence from the wiretap could be used in the trials of the defendants. It was a clear victory for Nina and the prosecution and likely meant that many of the defendants would be pleading guilty. After the judge ended the hearing, the marshals began leading the dejected cartel members out of the courtroom.

Nina met Xana back at the training center and gave her the good news. She let her know the decision was a big step in the right direction, but was not a guarantee Xana wouldn't have to testify at individual trials in the future.

"So, what are you going to do now, Xana?"

"I haven't the slightest idea."

"Good. Because Vic told me this morning that he and Doc have arranged to scatter Jake's ashes near Rathdrum in a few days—they've been putting it off because of the hearing. Maybe you can travel up with us?"

"I wouldn't miss it for anything."

CHAPTER 15

There were six people in Doc's G-wagon as he drove from Coeur d'Alene to Rathdrum. Doc and his wife were in the front and Vic, Nina, and Xana were in the back. The sixth person had been purified and reduced by fire, and, now in the form of ashes, was contained within a wooden box held carefully by Vic. The box was one Jake had made in his shop and had given to Vic a few years ago.

Doc drove to the Rathdrum Mountain Trail parking area, and everyone got out of the vehicle. Spring was on its way in northern Idaho, but it was still cold and the group had taken care to dress warmly—they had some hiking to do. Jake's will had stipulated his ashes to be scattered on Rathdrum Mountain, at a spot that overlooked the Rathdrum prairie. A specific spot wasn't mentioned, so one of the group's tasks was to find such a location. They started walking along the trail, which at the start was wide enough to accommodate vehicles. The trail's gradual ascent was not difficult, but enormous trees kept most of the sunlight from reaching the ground and it took everyone a while to warm up. After a little more than an hour, they found a possible location that had a view of the prairie—they felt they could do better and continued. After passing a couple more spots like the first one, they finally walked into a larger clearing that had a full, sweeping view of the landscape below.

"I think Jake would like this a lot, but he wouldn't want to be this close to the trail," said Vic. "Let's move across the slope until we're out of view from anyone passing by." They moved a few dozen yards from the trail and found a flat area with a fallen tree and two large rocks they could sit on. They were silent for a while, then Vic opened the box and tipped some of the ashes to the ground. They took turns scattering the ashes—Xana was crying as she took the box and some of her tears mixed in with the ashes. She didn't think it was a bad thing. When they were done and the box was empty, they sat for a while and took in the view of the prairie. After a few minutes they got up and walked back to the car.

Once they were inside the G-wagon, they decided to have lunch at a restaurant on Rathdrum's Main Street. When they were finished, Vic mentioned that Jake's attorney had requested they stop by his office in Coeur d'Alene. They drove to the office and filed into a conference room. The attorney greeted them and, after introductions, gave them some surprising news: Jake had left the entirety of his estate to Vic, Doc, and Xana. Once the estate was settled and after taxes, they each would net about four million dollars.

Zeke had not been in a good mood since he left Portland. When he was in the Mexican Marines, he'd been proud of his skills and felt like he was doing things for the betterment of his country. He didn't have much money but found solace in his duty and in his kinship with other members of the military. Since his retirement and recruitment to the cartel, there was no duty and no kinship: Everything was about money. He liked money, but when he looked at himself in the mirror he always felt a burdening sense of disappointment. While he'd been on active duty, he'd spoken to his mother frequently and always entertained her with his tales of military life and the funny things that had happened. Things were different now. He only spoke to her when she called him: There was no way he was going to tell her what he was actually doing, so he lied and told her he was working for a construction company and was always very busy, always on the road, sometimes in places that had no cell phone service. Zeke could tell by her voice that she knew something was wrong, but knew if he told her the truth she would worry incessantly and try to convince him to leave the cartel. Accordingly, he rarely answered her calls, knowing that every time they were on the phone he'd be subjected to a barrage of questions he didn't want to answer. He hadn't seen her in person for years but remembered the simple life he'd had as a child, with his beautiful mother and his soft-spoken father. As a young adult he had rejected life on the farm, but now wished he could go back to it. That wish drove him to continue to try to find Xana: If he could get the cash for bagging her, he could go back to his mother, make sure she had an easy life, and set them both up for the future.

He felt the solitary life of a sniper and cartel operative suited him well in some respects, but it had many drawbacks—chief among them being that it was impossible to have a girlfriend or wife. It seemed like everywhere he went were married couples with their children and seeing them tugged at something within him. Was it too late for him to get married, maybe start a family? He wasn't sure.

A couple days later Zeke met his controller in a busy restaurant in Las Vegas. His controller was filling him in on developments with the cartel.

"Well, there was a big court hearing over in Phoenix and, despite the amount of money we've shelled out for attorneys over the last few months, our side lost. The little bitch Xana was there, testifying against everyone. Now, a lot of our associates are probably going to negotiate for the best deal they can get and spend some time in jail. The ones who were able to make bail are already talking about returning to Mexico, but that's no guarantee of freedom either. All in all, it's been a real nightmare. There's one bit of good news for someone, though, maybe you."

"What's that?"

"They've increased the reward for capturing or killing Xana from two to five million. What's the status of your efforts to find her? The last I heard was that you found Xana's phone number but that we are blocked from getting its location."

"Yes, and it's a real shame because of what it took to get that number." He shuddered a little as he again remembered the feel of Chloe's hands clinging to his forearms. "I have no idea where she is. The only lead I have left is the address where that physician lives, but it would take some time and effort to watch his place. I don't think we should try to raid his house unless there is no other choice—so far he's killed everyone who's gone up against him."

"I don't know what to make of that, he's a conundrum, that one. Not very doctor-like, is he, downright unapproachable."

"Five million dollars, though…I'll tell you what, if I can borrow the guy who helped me with the Connor hit, I'll keep an eye on the physician's house for a few days. There's only a slim chance of anything developing from it, but you never know."

"Okay, but I'll take ten percent of the reward if you get her."

"Deal."

Two days later, Zeke was in Coeur d' Alene, planning with his helper. He'd instructed his helper to rent a minivan that had sliding back doors and rear seats that folded into the floor, to stock it with food and water, and to have it full of fuel at all times. Zeke didn't think his Camry was known to the police at all, so he planned on using it for the surveillance—it blended in well and was utterly reliable. Once the minivan was set up to Zeke's satisfaction, he took a drive past the physician's house in his Camry. There were no vehicles to be seen, so he left the area. When he made a second pass three hours later, he was startled to see a white 4Runner with Nevada license plates parked in front of the house: He knew his chances of finding Xana had just improved dramatically. He found a parking spot and called his controller.

"Hey, I just made a pass by the doctor's house and there's a 4Runner with Nevada plates sitting right out in front. Remember Nina Vasquez's boyfriend who lives in Vegas? I'm pretty sure this is his rig, and if he's here, Vasquez and Xana could be with him."

"Okay, what do you want to do?"

"Well, I know our bosses have a green light on the two cops, but there's not a giant reward for them like there is for Xana." He let that thought sink in. "I'd like to get more people, back off a little, and see if we can spot Xana in the car. If that happens, I'll make a plan to get her. I'd like to get two more operators over here, good ones that can think on the fly. If she's here, we may only get one shot at her."

"I have two good ones in Yakima right now that I can send over, but it will take them a few hours to get there."

"Have them come over in separate cars, and they should plan on living out of the car for a week or so. If this rig leaves town, we aren't going to have time to deal with checking in and out of hotels. So, food, water, clothing, weapons, they should know the drill."

"I'll have them on the way."

Zeke pulled up a map of the area and thought hard for a few minutes. It seemed unlikely the visitors would be staying at the house long term; they would probably head back south within a week. He knew he'd rather make his move while they were on the road: There were a lot of ex-cops and ex-military in Coeur d'Alene, as well as a very competent police department. With that in mind, he looked at the logical routes a driver would take to get to I-90 from the physician's house and leave town. There were two strong possibilities—he scouted both routes and determined the best places to watch for the 4Runner. He set up at one, and directed his helper to the other. When the other two operators arrived, he gave them assignments to back up each location and told everyone to settle in for a long wait. The first night passed quietly with no movement from the 4Runner. The next morning it left the house with one occupant—Zeke's team followed it efficiently but broke off when it returned to the house after making a trip to a grocery store. It was a good practice run, and the team was getting used to communicating with each other by conference cell-phone calls. There was no activity for the remainder of the day. At about five o'clock the next morning, however, they spotted the 4Runner as it headed towards I-90. As the 4Runner made a quick stop for fuel, the team was able to observe two people in front and one in back. Zeke was encouraged by the news but tempered his enthusiasm: If the vehicle contained Vasquez, her boyfriend, and Xana, as he suspected, getting to Xana was going to be extremely dangerous. He didn't care to remember all the cartel members who had died going up against the three.

What Zeke wanted was to improve his team's odds by getting to Xana while she was away from the other two. He wasn't sure how to accomplish that but decided to wait for an opportunity before risking an all-out assault on the vehicle.

His team followed the 4Runner from a distance as it crossed into Washington State, headed south through the Tri-Cities area, and then into Oregon. It stopped briefly for fuel and food in Baker City, and Zeke's team did the same. The long drive continued as the 4Runner eventually crossed back into Idaho, skirted past the Boise area, and headed towards Twin Falls. Once in Twin Falls, it pulled into a large hotel, but Zeke's team had no opportunities to take any action. They spread out around the perimeter of the hotel and settled in for a long night. Zeke assigned four-hour shifts in which they alternated watching and sleeping. At around six the next morning, the 4Runner was back on the road, and they again followed it as it made its way south into Nevada. Zeke was beginning to feel a little pressure building in his mind, and he wondered if they should just converge on the vehicle and try to kill everyone while it was on the lonely Nevada highway. He knew that had been tried before on this very same 4Runner, with fatal results for the cartel operators. He decided again to wait for an opportunity.

His patience finally paid off in Ely. The 4Runner pulled into a small mini mart for fuel, and one of the operators noticed that the restrooms were in the rear of the building, with outside entrances. Zeke watched as a woman he recognized as Vasquez walked to the rear of the building—he figured Xana would be headed that way next. He hurriedly parked his car and got into the minivan with its driver. After a minute, the others reported seeing Vasquez leave the restroom; they then saw Xana enter. Zeke had the driver slowly pull to the back of the building and wait nearby with one of the van's sliding doors left open. He quietly walked to the hinge side of the door to the women's room, waiting. At the instant it opened he punched Xana hard on the side of the jaw and pulled her into the minivan. He ran back to retrieve her purse, then got back into the van and closed the sliding door.

He told the driver to slowly leave the lot and to get back on the highway as he wrapped Xana's wrists with tape. Then, he told the other drivers to move his vehicle away from the mini mart and to await further instructions. Patting Xana down, he found a cell phone in her back pocket and tossed it out the window, then located a small pistol in a shoulder holster which he removed and tossed towards the back of the van. He quickly checked her purse for further weapons but didn't see any. After a minute, he saw her awakening as she looked up at him with hate in her eyes.

Xana struggled to think clearly as she came to. Her jaw hurt and she couldn't move her arms. As she opened her eyes, she saw dark blue carpeting and sensed motion. Fighting back the urge to vomit, she realized she was in a moving vehicle and that her hands were restrained behind her back. She felt her back pocket for her phone, but it was gone. After closing her eyes again, she waited until she could think clearly, then opened them. She now recognized her purse on the floor, just a couple feet from her. It looked like she was on the floor of a small van, and she could see the feet of a man sitting across from her. The rear floor area of the van was flat, and it appeared the back seats had been folded into the floor. She thought of Nina and Vic, hoping they were unharmed and wondering if they had any idea what had happened to her. She then remembered her Garmin was in her purse, turned off. If she could turn it on, Nina would at least know where she was. She sat up, moving about a foot closer to her purse as she did so, and looked up at the man.

"You look like the kind of turd who would rise to the top of the cartel's toilet bowl. Are you the one who killed Jake Connor?" She wanted him angry and thinking, so he wouldn't pay attention to her hands. She wiggled around as if her arms were hurting, getting a few inches closer to the purse as she did so.

"Regrettably, yes. I took no joy in it."

Xana locked eyes with him and leaned in. "Then I'm going to kill you. What about Chloe, I suppose you've met her now too?" She leaned back, gaining a couple more inches. She just had a little further to go.

"I'm afraid so, but Chloe is still alive. I regret my time with her, if you must know."

Xana kicked at him, a move he easily blocked but which positioned her hands so she could grab the edge of her purse. She folded her legs in front of her to block his view and slowly slid the purse behind her and began reaching in for the Garmin. "How much do you get for me?"

"Evidently there was some type of court hearing you were recently at—after the hearing, the reward jumped to five million dollars."

She had the Garmin and was pressing the side button to turn it on. She knew it would attempt to begin tracking almost immediately. The bad news was that it performed best when in an open area with no obstructions. From her purse, and while inside a moving vehicle, she knew it would take much longer to send information Nina could access. She held the little device away from the purse and pointed towards a window as much as she could. "Is that dead or alive, or what?"

"Either, but everyone really just wants you dead. So that's where this is headed, I'm sorry to say."

"Then why am I sitting here talking to you?"

"Sometimes it's all about location." He turned to speak to the driver. "Speaking of which, take this next dirt road to the right, it looks as good as any other."

Vic and Nina had a few moments of panic when they realized Xana was gone, but their police instincts soon took over. Nina called for emergency location information for Xana's phone, and was quickly advised the phone was stationary along Highway 6 leading west from Ely. Vic began driving in that direction but found nothing when they arrived where the phone had been pinged, about two miles west of Ely.

"Okay," said Nina. "We have one more chance. If she has her Garmin turned on, I can still get her location." She began working furiously on her cell phone. "Got her," she said, after a minute. "She's in a car; I can tell by how quickly she's moving. Clearly she's been kidnapped. Keep driving forward, while I check something out."

Vic could see that she was accessing topographical maps of the area and knew their experience with thru hiking and understanding of terrain was about to pay off.

"All right, I have an idea. Up ahead in just a couple of miles there are a series of canyons that lead off to the right. They've driven up one of them, but the canyon right before it has a road as well, that roughly parallels the one they're on. Rather than charge them from behind, where they'll see us all the way in, let's take the earlier canyon, keep pace with them, then climb the ridge and drop down on them once they stop."

"On it. Just tell me where to turn."

She consulted her phone. "Take this next road and step on the gas, they're a mile ahead of us. They're probably looking for a remote place to kill her and dump her body."

"Okay. Maybe you can hop in the back seat and load the rifles I have in the back. There's an AR and a .308."

Nina accomplished that quickly then was back in the front seat, checking her phone again.

"They've stopped a half mile ahead of us. We need to haul ass up there and get over the ridge."

Vic drove as quickly as he could. When Nina told him to stop, he pulled over, turned the 4Runner off, and jammed the keys in his pocket. They grabbed the rifles and began running to the top of the ridge. It was a forested area, though not thick, and there were patches of snow still on the ground. It was a few hundred yards to the top, and they were both breathing heavily when they reached the crest. They could see a van below them, at which two men were fighting to pull Xana out through a sliding side door on the passenger side. She was putting up a ferocious battle and they saw one man's head snap back as she delivered a kick to his face.

Vic pointed to a group of trees about four hundred yards from the van. "Let's get to those trees while they're fighting, then I can take them out with the .308." Their lungs still pumping from the ascent, they began running downhill as quickly as they could. Along the way, they knocked a few rocks loose that loudly rolled down the hill, but the men below took no notice. When they reached the trees, Vic unfolded his bipod and lay down on the ground behind the rifle. As he made a turret adjustment for the distance, he saw that the men had finally extracted Xana from the van and were dragging her away from it by the hair, towards a section of terrain that sloped downward from the road.

Vic was comfortable taking a chest shot from the trees, but wished he had more time to recover from his exertion: It was difficult to hold his breath, and his heavy breathing caused his scope to move way too much. Nevertheless, when he saw one of the men draw a pistol he knew it was time. He clamped down on his breathing, centered his reticle on the man's chest, and pulled the trigger. The man dropped, his shirt immediately turning red. Vic worked the bolt and searched for the other man in the scope but just had a fleeting glance as he disappeared behind the van.

"He grabbed something out of the van and ran down to the bottom of the canyon. Let's let him go and get to Xana," said Nina.

They moved quickly to Xana, and Vic cut the tape on her arms with his pocketknife.

"That fucker that ran," Xana was saying, "He admitted to me that he's the one who killed Jake." Vic's head jerked up at the mention of Jake, and he involuntarily started down the canyon.

"Hold up Vic," said Nina. "Our first responsibility is to guard Xana, and we don't know if any others are headed this way. We'll let the Nevada cops go after him. I'll call 911 in just a minute." Vic knew she was right and reluctantly walked back to her. Nina asked Xana for a description of the man. Xana provided accurate details of him, down to the type of shoes he was wearing.

"And I heard the dead guy calling him Zeke," she said.

They retreated to the trees from which Vic had taken the shot as they waited for the authorities. It was a long day as they worked with the local and state police. There was a combined effort from several agencies to locate the fleeing man, but by late in the evening he'd not been located.

CHAPTER 16

Zeke saw a glint in the tree line above him and knew exactly what it was. He sprinted to the far side of the van where he stuffed two water bottles, some snacks, and a stocking cap into two grocery bags, then took off running to the bottom of the canyon. Along the way he heard the shot he was sure killed the other man—it gave speed to his legs, and he knew his first priority was to simply put a lot of distance between himself and the van. After running hard for about a half mile he settled into a smooth, distance-consuming run he knew he could keep up for several hours. It would have helped, he thought to himself, if Xana had not kicked him in the face, as he suspected his nose was broken. He couldn't breathe through it very well and there was blood all the way down to his chin. Before long he reached Highway 6, where he waited for a lull in the vehicle traffic, then dashed across to the south without being seen.

Zeke had a heart-stopping moment when he patted his jacket pocket for his phone—it wasn't there, and he realized he'd left it in the van. Cursing himself for his foolishness, he resigned to somehow getting by on his own. At least, he told himself, he still had his .45 in its shoulder holster under his left arm. He felt the pistol bouncing along with every step, as did the two extra magazines under his right arm.

Two hours later, he continued to run and to pile up the distance. He was making good time in the terrain, which was sparsely covered with small trees and only occasional bits of snow. Ahead of him, the thin ridgeline he was running just below continued to the south, and he figured he should stick to its canyons for the time being. His two biggest worries were dogs and drones. Zeke knew dogs, if left to themselves, could run him down. But he didn't have to outrun the dogs, he only had to outrun the dog handlers, and it would take an exceptional handler to be able to keep pace with him.

Drones were another matter entirely: Zeke knew they could be his downfall. His best bet, he believed, was to travel farther and faster than anyone could anticipate, and he knew he was well on the way to doing just that. It was already late in the afternoon, so Zeke planned on running or walking through most of the night. The bad news was that he'd already downed one of his two water bottles but was still quite thirsty. He'd also eaten half the snacks he had grabbed from the van. He decided to start rationing his water to just a couple of sips each hour. He fought back a feeling of desperation and panic and continued on, still running as the sun set. As it became darker, he was forced to slow down to a quick walk—he scanned the horizons and saw that the moon was about to rise. In the far distance to the right, he could see headlights of cars travelling along a highway. Zeke believed he was looking at Highway 318, which he'd driven a few times in the past few years.

If memory served him, the tiny town of Lund would be up ahead, and he knew he should consider the town as a possible source of provisions.

As he walked along, he was grateful for the dim light the three-quarter moon began to provide. However, he also realized he'd been sweating quite a bit and the moisture was making him cold in the rapidly decreasing temperatures. He pulled on his stocking cap and felt a little better, but the difficulties of his situation continued to weigh on his mind—he simply kept walking, knowing every mile he put behind him was a victory.

At about one A.M., he could see the lights of the town he presumed was Lund along the highway ahead of him. A couple of hours later, it was directly off to his right, about five miles away. Should he go there? He weighed his options: His second water bottle was almost dry, and he only had a couple snacks left. He didn't recall any towns to the south of Lund for a long way. He also didn't remember seeing any grocery stores in Lund, but money talked and he had plenty of cash on him. Perhaps he could convince a resident to sell him a few things for the right price. He also knew he could break into someone's house, and he kept that possibility open in his mind. It was, indeed, quite a mess he'd ended up in.

With sore feet, he began to climb down from the ridge towards the flatter terrain along the highway. When he was about halfway down, he saw a primitive road off to his left as well as a little shack at the end of it. The shack was a wonderful sight to behold, and he walked directly to it. The door was secured with a flimsy hasp and padlock, which he defeated with a heavy blow from his shoulder. Once inside he couldn't see much but rummaged around and eventually found a lighter and a small candle. The interior of the shack was very simple: It simply consisted of a bench on one side of the space, and an army cot with a dark gray blanket on the other. On top of the bench, however, were two one-gallon jugs of water, some canned goods, an empty beer bottle, and a partially consumed bag of beef jerky. Zeke hoisted one of the gallon jugs to his lips and downed almost half of it, then used a little water to clean the dried blood from his face. He moved the candle closer to the canned goods and saw there were four cans of black beans, four cans of peaches, and one small can of coffee. The coffee can was already open, and the others had pull-tabs on top. He found some used plastic spoons, opened one can of black beans and one of peaches, and began wolfing it all down. It tasted like heaven to him, and he drank all the juice from both cans. He scooped up some of the coffee with the spoon, poured it in the empty beer bottle, added some water and, after a minute, sampled the contents: It was gritty but drinkable, though he had to keep spitting out the grounds. He began to feel a slight caffeine boost, for which he was grateful as he wanted to keep moving for several more hours. Zeke filled his empty water bottles from the half-consumed gallon jug and placed them, along with all the food and beer bottle, into his doubled grocery bags. He'd been eyeing the blanket and cot because they were intoxicatingly inviting to him...but instead of lying down he rolled up the blanket, tied the roll with some cord he found, then made a long loop with more cord so he could sling the blanket around one shoulder, vagabond-style.

After slinging the blanket, Zeke picked up the remaining gallon of water with one hand, his bags with the other, and started back up the ridge. He felt considerably better after taking in the food, water, and coffee, but knew he'd sleep like the dead once he found a place to bed down for the day. Once he made it almost to the top of the ridge he continued walking generally to the south, as the terrain allowed. The heavy items in his hands quickly became an annoyance, both because of the weight and because they tended to compress his upper arms into his pistol and magazines. He knew the load would get lighter with his consumption, so he simply pushed on, as quickly as he could. The sweat had dried from his body, and as long as he kept moving he felt only a slight chill.

Dawn came in slowly with a startling range of colors off to his left. Zeke figured he was twenty-five to thirty drone miles from where he started, but much more in actual hiking miles. His feet were hurting badly. He started looking for some kind of rock outcropping he could hide underneath—a cave would be better, but he knew his chances of finding one were slim. After half an hour he found a tree growing next to a large rock, with a bit of hollow space in between. He spread half the blanket out in the space, crawled in, and pulled the other half over him. One of the water bottles sufficed for a pillow and he curled up, shivering just a little. Within a minute he was asleep.

Sunlight in his eyes awakened him, and he checked the position of the sun—it was about an hour until dusk. He smelled the air and listened for a minute, but didn't notice anything unusual. He wiggled his toes to get a preview of how his feet were doing—they were a little sore, but much better than before he'd slept. Finding his plastic spoon, he put a little coffee into his beer bottle and added a few ounces of water. After the cold brew had sat for a few minutes, he opened another can of beans and peaches and had a meal, while considering his next move. He had enough food and water for a couple days, but then he would be in trouble. There was very little, as he could recall, in the way of civilization for a long distance south of Lund, but thought he remembered some type of wildlife area about thirty miles toward Vegas that offered fishing. Where there was fish, there would be water, and maybe even some food. And more to his liking, there could be people there from whom he could buy supplies and perhaps pay to use a cell phone.

It was the only plan he could come up with. He decided to walk about twenty miles the first night, then scout around and find the wildlife area on the second night. As he was about to crawl out of his blanket, he heard a low-flying plane approaching—he covered his head with the blanket and waited for it to pass. Were there people in the plane trying to find him? He wasn't sure but waited until it was fully dark to pack up and head out. His legs ached, forcing him to gimp along for the first half mile until they warmed up and he could use his full stride. The main ridge he was following seemed to be gaining in elevation, and he decided to move to a lower level—the wildlife area was on the other side of the highway, and he figured he should stay somewhat close to the flat terrain that Highway 318 followed. He tried to stay about ten percent above the level of the roadway, so he could hide in the canyons if need be.

Zeke wished he had some way of knowing the status of any efforts to find him. His life would be a lot easier if he knew what was going on. In the meantime, he simply kept putting one foot in front of the other, while trying to be aware of what was going on around him. Traffic on the highway was sparse, but the passing vehicles made it easy for him to stay oriented and on track. After covering about twenty miles, he began looking for his next place to sleep. As the eastern skies were just beginning to tinge from black to gray, he followed a torturous canyon uphill for about a mile. He found a conveniently overhanging rock, which promised to provide him with much better concealment than he'd had the first night. After having some jerky and water, he spread his blanket underneath the rock and crawled in.

Several hours later, he woke up. His face itched, and he rubbed the stubble on his jaw as he began to make his plan for the night. He knew he had to be getting close to the wildlife area, and didn't want to overshoot it. As he had his beer-bottle coffee and canned food, he decided he'd have to risk hiking much closer to the highway for his third night out. He had a vague recollection of a roadside sign for the turnoff to the area, so he decided to head south and to simply watch for the sign. If he could locate the area and get situated in the dark, he could assess things when it started to get light. With that in mind, he packed up, walked down the canyon, and moved closer to the highway as darkness fell. His water containers were almost empty, and his food almost gone. But the flatter terrain and lighter load made it easy for him to cover distance, something his feet and legs seemed to appreciate.

Zeke continued to get closer to the highway and started looking for the rectangular sign he thought he remembered. When he was about sixty yards or so from the roadway he could make things out fairly well in the moonlight, and passing vehicles helped as well. He knew he was well outside the throw of headlights, unless someone happened to turn off the road at just the wrong time. Finally, at about three A.M., he saw a sign near a well-travelled road that led off the highway to the west. When there was a break in traffic he ran up to the sign: *Kirch Wildlife Area*, it read, along with an arrow pointing to the west. He darted across the highway and began following the road to the wildlife area but staying in the scrub and well to the south. After a bit he encountered a few houses and a dog began barking at him; he simply increased his speed and kept walking as the road turned toward the south. There was some groundwater along the way, but he hesitated to drink any of it until he could take a closer look in the daytime. He'd been sickened by water before and certainly couldn't afford to be ill now. After a couple of miles, he saw three cars parked just off the road and he knew what they were: Car campers.

Zeke was a reluctant aficionado of car camping: He didn't like it but sometimes had to do it. He had respect for those who could live out of their cars, trucks, and vans for months at a time and had emulated their methods many times. Car campers often talked of being free from permanent physical structures as they lived their lives, but Zeke had lived the truth and knew that car camping was dead-ass boring most of the time. Plus, in a small car like his Camry, even simple things like relieving himself required thought, planning, and ingenuity. Many campers were short on cash, and Zeke decided to approach one of them to buy supplies during the daylight hours. He found a little hollow in the ground amongst some boulders, unrolled his blanket, and went to sleep.

He'd told himself to wake up early, and he sat up in his blanket at ten A.M. After having a little food and coffee with the last of his water, he walked over to where he'd seen the campers. There was only one car left, and in a folding lawn chair next to it sat a man Zeke thought looked suitable for his purposes: The man was in his late fifties, with a wrinkled face and a bloodshot, alcoholic nose. There was already an empty beer can under the chair. He approached the man and leaned back on the front quarter panel of his car. He could see two cases of bottled water in the back seat.

"Morning," he said. "Been here long?"

"Just a couple days. It's been nice and quiet. How are you?"

"Well, I've had a tough time. My girlfriend kicked me out of our van two days ago, and I played hell just trying to get here." He shook his head. "I could call my brother to come pick me up, but my phone's in the van. So, I'm wondering if I can buy some supplies from you, maybe borrow your phone?" He showed the man a hundred-dollar bill.

"I don't see why not, we have to look out for each other." He began to show Zeke what he had in the car. Zeke ended up with twelve bottles of water, some assorted food items, and a canvas sack that was better than the doubled plastic grocery bags he'd been using. Then the man handed Zeke his phone, and he walked a short distance away from the man with it. He first opened the phone's map program to confirm where he was and saw that the small town of Ash Springs was the first town of any size to the south. There wasn't much to Ash Springs, he recalled, but it did have a sizable gas station that was a popular location for truckers to sleep during the night. The town was on Highway 93, just a little south from where Highway 318 intersected it, about sixty miles away. He texted his controller a message that simply read *911* so his following voice call would be answered. Then he called and gave his controller a quick update of all that had transpired. He requested a pickup just north of Ash Springs at six A.M. in three days. That settled, he gave the man his phone back, gathered his items, and made his way back to his camping spot. He hadn't wanted to get picked up at the wildlife area in case the man or anyone else made a connection between him and the shooting up north—it was better, he thought, to have a little more time and distance from the shooting. He knew he'd be safe out in the brush now that he had food and water again.

Zeke took a nap at his hidden campsite, waking up just as the sun was going down. He had sixty miles to cover in three nights, but he wasn't worried about it—he had enough food and water, he had only to follow the highway to his destination, and he wasn't going to be climbing too much anymore.

At six A.M. on the appointed day, Zeke was concealed in some bushes just north of Ash Springs. He was a little concerned about how he'd recognize the operative sent to pick him up. He needn't have worried; just after six he saw his trusty white Camry slowly creeping towards him on the shoulder of the highway. When it reached him he jumped up, waved at the driver, and climbed in the back seat. The driver turned out to be one of the operatives from Yakima who had helped with the effort to capture Xana. Zeke asked the man to head a few miles south towards the town of Alamo, where he knew there was a good-sized store. He was happy to be back in civilization.

CHAPTER 17

Nina sat in her Phoenix office, reviewing the report her Intelligence Analysts had put together regarding Ezequiel "Zeke" Mendoza. They had done a stellar job: The report outlined his humble childhood, his entry into and accomplishments as a Mexican Marine, and his recruitment and activities as a Manzanillo cartel operative and sniper. The acquisition of Zeke's cell phone from the van in Nevada played a key role in the detailed nature of the report—the analysts had put together a flow chart of his contacts, as well as a timeline of his geographic locations. Already, parts of the report had been forwarded to law enforcement in Portland to assist them in the investigation into the assault of the woman known as Chloe. In Idaho, Zeke now had arrest warrants from State and Federal authorities for the murder of Jake Connor and several other crimes. Analysis of DNA recovered from the phone was also in progress.

Zeke's home address in the Dallas area had also been established, and authorities there had agreed to surveil the house for a few days in case Zeke showed up. Nina had no way of knowing for sure if Zeke was still alive, but her gut told her he was yet among the living. His body hadn't been found, and he seemed to be the type who could survive most anything.

After being picked up by his fellow operative in Ash Springs, Zeke once again found himself in a Las Vegas hotel. His controller told him to take some time to recuperate and to change his appearance a little—Zeke bought some new clothes and had a stylist give him a short, plain haircut. After a week, he and his controller met at a quiet restaurant in Henderson, just a few miles east of Las Vegas.

"Well," his controller was saying. "Everyone is pretty impressed with how you made it through the desert all those miles; your legend continues to grow. What's not so good is that the little bitch Xana is still alive, and now she'll be even harder to get."

"It was a close call, and a lot of work was ruined at the last second. I was sure I was going to be five million richer, except for your cut, of course. Maybe we'll have another chance with her somehow."

"Let me know if you come up with something. In the meantime, because they have your phone, we need to assume you now have warrants and make some changes right away. First, we are taking back your Camry. Sorry, I know you like it. Do you have a preference for your next ride?"

"Definitely another Toyota. How about an off-road Tacoma with a dark gray color? Xana and all her buddies all drive four-wheel drive rigs, so I might as well join the club."

"We'll see what we can do. Next, we're going to sell your Dallas house and move you here to Vegas. We'll have to figure out what to do with the contents in case the cops are watching. Is there anything incriminating in there we should know about?"

Zeke couldn't think of anything incriminating, but there were some letters from his mother, some cash, and some weapons he didn't want to lose. "No, but there are some small items I'd like to get out before the place is cleaned up."

"You should assume the place is being watched and be clever about it if you insist on going there. Don't say I didn't warn you. A couple last things." He pulled a phone and a set of new identification cards from his pocket and handed everything to Zeke. "I'll let you get new chargers for the phone if you need them. Try not to lose this one."

"I'll do my best."

"All right. I'll let you know when the truck and your house are ready. In the meantime, be careful."

"Will do."

Back at his hotel, Zeke considered his options for the Dallas house. He definitely wanted the letters from his mother back—but he also had two hundred thousand dollars in cash hidden in the place, as well as some weapons he'd spent a lot of time sighting in. He borrowed a minivan from another operator and drove to a sporting goods store, where he purchased a monocular thermal device. On the way back to his hotel he fueled the van and made sure it was ready for a long drive. Once back in his room he packed a large duffle bag and went to bed.

The next morning, he was up early and on the road. He made it to Albuquerque by midafternoon, got himself a room and some food, and slept. The following day he drove to Dallas and rented another room not far from his old house. Zeke set his alarm for two A.M. and went to bed—he awoke before the alarm went off, redressed, and removed a blanket and a frameless backpack from the duffle bag. After stuffing the blanket into his backpack, he put his new monocular device into his pocket, walked to the minivan, and drove to his former neighborhood. He parked the van on a residential street one block over from his house, so he could see his backyard fence from his parking spot. Exiting the van, he turned on the thermal device, concealed it in his hand, and walked towards the corner of the street his house faced. As he approached the corner, he held the device to his eye and began examining the cars that were parked near his house—sure enough, there was one vehicle about a half-block from his place that was giving off a heat signature. Zeke didn't get any closer, but assumed it was law enforcement and knew he'd have to enter his house from the back. After returning to the minivan, he pulled on the backpack and walked toward his backyard fence. He had to walk through the yard of the house directly behind his property, but there was no alternative—he simply had to be quiet. The cedar fence dividing the two properties groaned loudly under his weight as he climbed over it, and he crouched in the darkness of his own yard for a few minutes to make sure he hadn't alarmed anyone.

When he felt he was in the clear, he walked to the back door and opened it with a key. Using only his phone's screen for light he first went to his desk, located the letters from his mother, and stashed them in his backpack. Next, he quickly went to the places where he had concealed cash and put it all in the backpack as well. Finally, he opened a gun safe in one of the spare bedrooms and from it removed four rifles and three pistols. The pistols fit in his backpack, but the rifles he simply carried in his arms. After exiting the house and relocking the back door, he returned to where he had crossed the fence. He could see it was going to be a challenge to get everything over the fence without making a lot of noise—he leaned the rifles up against the fence, then climbed up until he could lift his backpack up, maneuver it over the fence, and lower it most of the way to the ground. He let go of it, and it made a soft clunk as it hit the ground. The rifles, he discovered, were long enough that he could grab them one at a time, lift them over the fence, and lean them against the other side without making any noise. He climbed over the fence, removed the blanket from the backpack, and wrapped the rifles up in it. The disguise wasn't much but might help a little if anyone saw him as he returned to the minivan. After shouldering the backpack, he picked up the rifles and moved to the vehicle. Within a minute he was driving back to the hotel.

After the most recent attempt on her life, Xana was in turn angered and relieved. It was truly exasperating how many times the cartel continued to come after her. She knew someday, if it kept up, her luck would run out and she would join the many who'd been plowed under.

She thought often of her poor aunt and uncle, both of whom had been killed by the cartel. She also thought of her mother—she'd mentally closed the door to her mother in the past, but now she had questions. Why had her mother turned out so poorly, when she'd come from a decent and respectable family? How had she become addicted to drugs and alcohol, and to live a lifestyle that seemed to be mostly just shacking up with one uninspiring man after another? Had her decline been the result of a single incident, or was it an accumulation of poor decisions? She didn't know the answer to any of her questions, and there was no one to ask. Xana wasn't even sure if her mother was still alive, but after some internet research discovered her mother had passed away a few years ago. Further research showed her mother had been buried in a family plot near Mexico City, along with Xana's aunt, uncle, and grandparents.

It all left her feeling unmoored, and to again question her identity and purpose. She decided to make a trip to Mexico City, thinking that perhaps she would feel a revelation or even a sense of closure if she were close to her family again.

The following week she walked up to her family's plot and read all the grave markers. She felt deep sorrow for her aunt and uncle, who'd been so kind to her and took her in when her mother had kicked her out. She felt sorrow for her mother as well, but it was the sorrow of what could have been, and what should have been. With her mother in the ground in front of her, she reflected on how she'd had to scrape by and rely on herself to survive, even as a very young girl. It wasn't fair, she knew. But had it prepared her to survive the years that were to come? Was her self-reliance, in fact, the very reason she was still standing on the ground, instead of lying next to her mother underneath it? She had to concede that it was, even if it had developed through carelessness and neglect.

She wanted some type of closure and again looked at the grave markers one by one. She told her grandparents and her aunt and uncle she loved them, then finally her eyes rested on her mother's gravestone. She grappled with what to say, and it took her a long few minutes to figure it all out. Then she looked at her mother's grave one last time.

"I forgive you, Mama," she said, and walked away.

CHAPTER 18

Nina looked across her desk at an attorney who had introduced himself as Antonio Sotero. He had requested an appointment with her a few days prior, stating he had some information regarding criminal activity which he wished to pass on to her. As was her habit, Nina had done some research on the man prior to the meeting: She'd discovered he was a defense attorney who had represented several members of the Durango cartel—rivals to the Manzanillo cartel she'd been investigating for over a year.

"Thank you for agreeing to meet with me," the man was saying. "You probably don't have high regard for defense attorneys, so I appreciate it."

"It depends on the defense attorney, Mr. Sotero. I have very good friends who do defense work, but they tend to be what I would call honest defense attorneys. But I have little use—or time—for the dishonest ones."

"Then I suspect we'll get along just fine. I'll get straight to the point. In my line of work, I sometimes learn of criminal matters that are likely to be of interest to law enforcement. I'd like to develop a way to get that kind of information to you on a timely but anonymous basis—I'm sure you understand, I have attorney-client privileges to contend with."

"Let me guess," said Nina. "The information you have in mind would pertain to the Manzanillo cartel, and not the cartel whose members you represent."

Sotero winced a little. "That's a harsh way of putting it. Surely you can understand that my clients wouldn't want to incriminate themselves."

Nina knew exactly what was going on. It wasn't unheard of for criminal organizations to attempt to use law enforcement to eliminate their competition. In this case, the Durango cartel had no doubt observed the large-scale arrests of Manzanillo cartel members by Nina's team and their federal partners—now they were looking to further attack a weakened foe, with hopes of enlarging and enriching their own enterprise.

It put Nina in a difficult situation. On one hand her team certainly could not be some type of partner with one criminal group to get rid of another criminal group. Plus, Sotero's information would always be suspect because his organization stood to gain if members of the Manzanillo cartel were arrested. On the other hand, there could be information provided by Sotero that absolutely should be acted upon: Information concerning the whereabouts of underage trafficking victims, for example. She told him as much.

"Look, I'm not going to be your partner in taking down the Manzanillo cartel, that just smells bad. All I can do is evaluate the information you provide on a case-by-case basis. As far as anonymity goes—we can deal with you the same as we would any other informant and not use your name in reports. But you need to know that if a judge tells me to provide your name, I'm going to give it. Surely the cartel could offer you protection if that happens."

"Likely so. And thank you, I understand what you are saying." He paused for a moment. "I've heard you have a special interest in helping trafficking victims. As a way of demonstrating the reliability of my information, I'd like to give you some details of a location here in Phoenix where a number of mixed-age girls are being prostituted." He proceeded to give her the information.

Nina told him that her team would check into it and, after a little more conversation, he left the office. She sat in her chair, digesting everything. All in all, Sotero had left her with an unpleasant feeling, but she knew the chance to save victims took precedence over her sensibilities. She instructed her team to investigate the location—they quickly established probable cause and served a search warrant on the place within a couple weeks. Several trafficking victims were found, including one underage girl who had been missing for over three years. Sometimes, Nina thought grimly, a deal with the devil could result in a positive outcome, after all.

Zeke, now that he was a full-time resident of Las Vegas, was coming to the slow realization that perhaps he didn't have the right personality to live there. For one thing, he didn't like gambling at all—he was more of a planner/doer, rather than a person who hoped chance would come his way. For another thing, he didn't like strip clubs: He'd gone to a few as a younger man, but they'd always made him feel like a failure at life, and his wallet was always greatly diminished when he left. And finally, Zeke drank liquor only sparingly and did no street drugs at all, so the party scene didn't hold much attraction for him.

It was becoming clear there really wasn't much to do in Las Vegas for someone like him. He eventually realized that during the cooler months there were a lot of interesting places to hike within a short distance of Vegas, and he took full advantage of them. In the evenings, to keep the boredom away, he began to indulge in something he had a long-standing interest in: Rock music.

While growing up, his parents had always listened to traditional Mexican music, and he still liked a lot of it. While in the Mexican Marines, however, rock music was always played in the gym as they cranked out their exercises, and he'd been a devotee of the genre ever since. He eventually found a small club, a bit off the Las Vegas strip, that featured live rock shows every weekend. Except for when he was on some assignment or other with the cartel, Zeke was often at the club on Friday and Saturday nights, nodding his head to the music. In the midst of it all, he always made it a point to keep his wits about him and to scan the crowd for trouble. As time went on, he began to recognize the regulars and to get a sense of the environment: Most of the customers seemed to be middle-aged and were simply there for the love of music—just like him.

Zeke wasn't really looking for another girlfriend, but he couldn't help but notice the attractive, single women who sometimes showed up for the music. There was one woman in particular he began to look forward to seeing—she was blonde, pretty, fit, and about forty years old, just a little younger than him. Sometimes she would be there by herself, but more often she was with a couple of other ladies, and they all had a lot of fun dancing in front of the stage. He and the blonde began nodding and smiling at each other in passing, and he thought he could see a glimmer of interest in her eyes.

One evening he spotted her sitting at the bar with an unoccupied stool next to her. He sat down at the stool and turned to her. "I'm Zeke," he said. "May I buy you a drink?"

"So formal, you are," she said with a grin. "But yes, you may. And my name's Jessie."

They talked for a few minutes about the bands that were playing that night, then her female friends arrived and she went to a different part of the club with them. The next weekend, however, he was standing by himself when she appeared at his side and handed him a beer.

"May I present you with a beer?"

"You certainly may, I appreciate it. How are you?"

"I'm doing great!"

They talked for a while until the first band started playing and it was too loud to talk. When the band finished their set, Jessie turned to him.

"I'm not crazy about the next bands. But I know where the best party in town is tonight, do you wanna go?"

"What is it?"

"It's a band playing at one of the off-strip casinos in the south end of town. I'm not sure I can explain it; you might just have to trust me a little bit." She gave him a sidelong look.

"A man would be a fool to turn down an invitation like that. Let's go, and I can drive us."

They got into his brand new, dark gray Toyota Tacoma and travelled through Las Vegas to the casino. It wasn't huge like some of the main strip resorts, but it was by no means a small place. Zeke parked on the fifth floor of the parking garage, and they walked inside. Jessie guided him to a large music venue on the main floor—he paid for their admission and they went inside. He wasn't sure what to expect, and it took him a minute to figure out what was going on. On stage, the band members were all dressed in comically exaggerated seventies costumes, but, as he listened, he realized they were truly first-rate musicians. They were playing rock hits from the seventies and eighties, each song sounding remarkably like the original. There was a huge dance area in front of the stage that was packed with throngs of people, all dancing to the nostalgic music of their youth. Everyone seemed to be having a great time, and the vibe of the place was not quite like anything he'd experienced before.

Jessie grabbed his hand, pulling him onto the dance floor, and began to dance, clearly in her element. Zeke didn't think he was a very good dancer, but the energy was overwhelming and he was soon caught up in it all. Jessie was a funny and athletic dancer and she kept him going, even doing a little dirty dancing with him here and there. When it was over they walked back to his Tacoma, the cool desert air blowing through the parking garage and cooling them down. They made it back to the rock club parking lot and she pointed out her vehicle, a sharp-looking Mercedes. He parked next to it, turned his vehicle lights off, and they leaned into each other, kissing for a couple minutes. Then she wrote her number down for him, told him she hoped she'd hear from him soon, and was gone. When he was sure her vehicle had started, Zeke left the parking lot and headed home. Maybe, he told himself, the feelings he'd had about his personality not being a good match for Las Vegas needed to be reconsidered.

When Jessie awoke the next morning, she picked up her phone and called her now-and-then boss. Antonio Sotero, attorney for the Durango cartel, answered.

"Jessie, what do you have for me?"

"Well, you know that Zeke dude from the Manzanillos we heard was showing up at the rock club? Well, I've been working him a little and last night we hung out, he drove me around and everything. And yeah, he's totally into me and yeah, it's him. I mean, I saw his ID when he was paying for something and it's a different name, but it's him for sure."

"You are good, you."

"Call me a mean bitch, but you show me a lonely man and I'll show you a man I can gut. I have to be careful with this one though, Antonio. He has the eyes of a killer, and it creeps me the fuck out."

"He is a killer, and you'd do well to remember that. Just keep it light as long as you can, and don't let the shine wear off."

"I'll try. What are my instructions?"

"Let's use him for intel for now, just try to see what he's up to. I'll need to talk to my associates about Zeke. In the meantime, do you remember that girl Xana from his group?"

"Ah yes, the legendary and scary Xana, turned turncoat."

"Word is Zeke has been trying to find her, to collect the five-million-dollar reward. If he figures out where she is, maybe you and I can move in and get that reward for ourselves."

"Well, he's not going to find her while he's staring at my ass in the nightclub. This shit's not easy, always these tricky complications."

"Well, you know what they say, if it was easy…"

"Anyone could do it."

CHAPTER 19

Jessica "Jessie" Ross was a Las Vegas girl through and through. She'd been pretty and popular all through school, then had graduated from UNLV with a journalism degree. A partier, her grades had not been good enough to land her a job in the competitive Vegas journalism market. However, a couple of her friends were making excellent money as cocktail servers in the mega-resorts along the Las Vegas strip, and they encouraged her to apply. In most parts of the country, a cocktail server was not considered a very high-paying job—but a server working at a high-end club in a fancy Las Vegas resort could positively rake in the money and was often set for life. Competition for the positions was intense but Jessie, who looked great in a tiny outfit and who had the gift of gab, outshined others and had an extremely lucrative gig while still in her early twenties.

Partying, again, was her downfall. Jessie liked both cocaine and ecstasy and used both while having off-the-job fun with her friends. While in her early thirties, she made the mistake one night of selling some extra cocaine she had to an undercover officer, and she was arrested and charged. She was able to avoid jail time, but the criminal charge cost her the server job. The whole situation infuriated her, because she didn't think the "fun" drugs she liked should be against the law in the first place; she only thought drugs such as heroin and fentanyl should be outlawed. She'd vaguely heard of drug related crime and murders, as well as the negative environmental effects of illegal drug production, but those problems weren't personal to her so she didn't care.

Jessie had made a lot of money during her ten-year career as a server—she had a condo in nearby Summerlin and a new Mercedes, both fully paid for, as well as a healthy bank account and some small investments. Her financial needs weren't acute, but she did try to bring in some extra cash as she could. Often, she worked as a model at the various trade shows in Vegas: Those who hired her were always well-pleased, whether she was in a bikini, motorcycle gear, or tactical getup. When the shows ended for the day, it was easy for her to get someone to buy her dinner and drinks. It was during such a dinner that she met Antonio Sotero, who also lived in Vegas and had been attending a car show. A smart man, he recognized the natural, easygoing talent Jessie seemed to have for influencing men and bending them around her finger. Sotero was invested in a company, featured at the car show, that made aftermarket fuel delivery and ignition systems for high-performance vehicles. While casually speaking to Jessie, he pointed out some competitors across the bar and let her know he'd make it worth her while if she could find out what technology the other company would be using in their products in the coming year.

Jessie liked the challenge and was utterly confident in her abilities. She approached the man in the group who looked the most hard-up for women, asked him if he knew the time, and began a conversation with him. It was a simple matter for her to feign interest in technicalities of engine performance during the conversation she guided the eager man through, and after an hour she knew everything there was to know about the company's tech plans. She pretended like she was getting a phone call, excused herself from the man, and gestured for Sotero to meet her in the next room over. She recounted what the man had told her in precise detail, even though she didn't really understand what it all meant. Sotero was amazed at what she'd been able to learn and gave her two thousand dollars in cash.

"This helps my company out more than you realize; now we know how to keep a jump ahead of the others."

"It was literally like falling off a log, men were trying to give me more information than that all day long. And don't forget, I even got you to buy me dinner."

"I'm aware. Listen, my friends and I have our fingers in quite a few things. If you're willing, maybe in the future we can send you on these types of scenarios again. What do you think?"

Jessie thought quickly. "Well, I'll listen, but to be honest, two grand is a little low. I mean, by the time I shower, put on my expensive clothes and makeup, do my hair, drive, pay for parking...a girl can't roll high for low money, you know. And no sex, I'm not a ho."

"I know you're not, and I wouldn't ask that. Why don't we set a minimum of five grand with the option of raising that amount, depending on how much time and effort it takes you."

"Sounds like a good time to me, as long as it's always in cash."

"Perfect, we'll be in touch."

"Okay, but aren't you forgetting something, Antonio?" She extended out the last vowel of his name in a playful manner.

"What do you mean?"

She stuck out her hand. "You still owe me three thousand dollars."

He gave her the money.

As the years went by, Jessie worked with Antonio on a variety of assignments. She became even more confident in her abilities and began to look forward to the work. She didn't really need the income, but the cash she received helped and she called it her "fun money"—it was used for trips, going out with her friends and for recreational drugs. Jessie mostly stayed true to her no-sex rule, but she often found that a little kissing and groping could go a long way towards success, so she took those instances in stride. Twice she actually did have full-on sex with her targets, but told herself she would have had sex with the men anyway. All in all, she thought it was quite funny that she got paid for flirting and simply carried on with her partying lifestyle. Just a Vegas girl doing Vegas things, she figured.

CHAPTER 20

Xana was climbing Rathdrum Mountain for the second time in just a matter of weeks. Alone this time, she was on a mission of personal redemption. Her trip to Mexico had allowed her to feel more at ease with the way she remembered her mother; now she wanted to try the same for her memory of Jake.

As she walked, she reflected on what he'd told her about his childhood, being in law enforcement, the tragic death of his wife and son, and the tailspin he'd been in for many years. Yet when she remembered her time with Jake he hadn't seemed to be a man in decline—she recalled how kind he'd been when she woke up in his house, the care and respect he'd shown for her, and how he'd done his best to protect her at the airport. She also considered how he'd been, clearly falling in love with her, as she'd nursed him back to health in Rathdrum. It was that part that gave her a disquieting feeling, made her wonder if she could have done better, shown a little more grace to a man who'd lost so much. She wasn't sure.

Eventually she reached the spot where the ashes had been scattered. Looking around, she couldn't see anything that looked like ashes, and knew he'd been reclaimed by the earth. She sat down on a rock, closed her eyes, and thought hard about what she wanted to say. Eventually she opened her eyes, took in the Rathdrum prairie that Jake had called home, and started to speak as tears formed in her eyes.

"My dear Jake. Thank you for saving my life and for taking such good care of me when I really needed it. I was just a stranger, yet I could feel the kindness flowing to me through your broken heart, and I'll never forget it. When I was with you I always felt safe, and that means more to me than you can imagine. But Jake, please forgive me for the way I was before I left your house, I know you wanted to connect with me more but I wasn't ready, I was trying to protect you. It was better between us during our late-night phone calls once I was beginning to figure myself out. I don't know if that was enough, and I'm sorry. You need to know that I love you, I always will, and I'll never forget you." Wracked with sobs, Xana leaned into the rock upon which she sat, her tears falling upon it as she cried uncontrollably. After several minutes she wiped away her tears and stood up. Her normal personality eased back into place.

"One more thing," she said. "We know who did this to you, and we're going after that mother*fucker*."

Nina sat in her office with Antonio Sotero, taking notes as he provided information about an individual who was a trafficker for the Manzanillo cartel. When he was finished he broached another subject with her, one that took her by surprise and gave her an emotional rush she had to fight to conceal.

"You may or may not have heard of a Manzanillo operative named Zeke," Sotero was saying. "He's the best they have, a former military guy who's made himself into a highly skilled sniper, killer, and all-around fixer. I can't tell you how many of our guys he's managed to drop over the years, both up here and in Mexico. He's a bit of a ghost in that he prefers to work alone; he only accepts help when he has to. He's been on our radar for some time and, while we are being honest, our attempts to go after him have not been successful. It wouldn't hurt our feelings in the slightest if American law enforcement were to take him into custody and put him away for a few decades. In fact, I've heard he may already have warrants out for his arrest?" He cocked an eyebrow at her.

"I can't comment on warrants, and we'd need to do some background on this guy in any case. Are you trying to tell me you have a way we could get to him, assuming he's wanted?"

"It's over in Las Vegas and not here in Phoenix, but yes, I do. It turns out Zeke and a female associate of mine have similar tastes in music—they connected at a little rock club over there and have just begun spending time together. She wants to get out already because he scares her, but I think we can work this to our mutual advantage."

"Is this woman a prostitute?"

"No, she's more like an informal spy. We've used her on many occasions to get information from men whose interests compete with ours."

"Is she being forced to help you somehow?"

"Lord no, she does it for the money and she's not shy about asking for it. With Zeke, initially she wanted to try to milk him for information about an ex-Manzanillo member named Xana, for whom there is a five-million-dollar reward—I won't ask you to comment on that. But now that she's spent time with Zeke and is scared, she wants to wrap it up somehow and move on—preferably with him dead or locked up. She's ready to cooperate with police, but I'll give you a heads up about something: She has an old drug delivery conviction she'll be asking for help to get rid of."

"Sometimes that's easier said than done. So, this guy could possibly be lured in with the oldest trick in the book. Are you sure this girl is up for it?"

"I would call her a woman, not a girl; she's all of forty. But gorgeous, and hell on wheels with the talk. Jessie is her name, and my money would be on her."

"If the information about Zeke turns out to be accurate, I'll need to deal with Jessie directly; you'll be cut out of it. I'll get back to you in a day or two."

"Sounds good."

A week later, Nina sat across a table from Jessie, in an office she had borrowed from the Las Vegas Metro Police. The woman was strikingly beautiful and had a carefree vibe about her—Nina pitied the men Jessie targeted in her work for Sotero. She asked Jessie to bring her up to date with what was going on between her and Zeke.

"Well, I've really only hung out with him twice—once we went to see a band in the south end, and then we had a couple drinks near my place in Summerlin. He's been nice enough both times, but I have to tell you that this dude scares me. It's his eyes. Have you ever had anyone look at you like you're a fly they could swat? He's kind of like that."

"That sounds uncomfortable. Do you have any future plans with him?"

"No. He's been calling though, and I've been dodging him. I should get back to him before too long."

"Okay, we'll figure something out soon. This next question I have to ask, because it could come up in court. Is there anything sexual going on with him?"

"No, not unless you consider making out and grab-assing to be sexual. He would, in a heartbeat, but I've been slow-walking it. That's all I normally do with people Antonio sends me to; I'm not a hooker."

"I know you're not, but I had to ask the question. I can tell you're scared of him, and I get it. But has he threatened you in any way, or normally carry any weapons?"

"No actual threats whatsoever, and no weapons that I know of. I probably would have felt it if he was armed. If I had to guess, I would say he probably has a gun in his truck. I mean, I can't imagine a person like him being without a gun, except for when they might get wanded by security."

"Makes sense to me. So Jessie, Mr. Sotero said you were interested in getting rid of a conviction you have; what's the deal with that?"

"It was a little over ten years ago, back when I was younger and dumber. My coworkers and I were at an after-hours party and yes, we were doing some lines. A guy I didn't know wanted to buy some blow and, like a dumb-ass, I sold a little to him. Barely any, but he was a cop, and he arrested me, and it cost me my job. If I help with Zeke, can you help me get rid of that conviction? It's been ten years, and I've been in no trouble since then."

"Ten years is a long time with no trouble. If this works out, I think I can help you petition the court to have the conviction sealed or expunged. I need to be upfront with you, only a judge can make the call, all we can do is ask. But I would say you have a good shot, ten years with no further arrests should mean something to a judge."

"It would mean a lot to me. Listen, however this works out, can we do it so I'm not right there when you arrest him? I can barely sleep, I keep thinking and worrying about getting shot."

"We'll do the absolute best we can to keep you safe."

Later that evening, Nina sat with Vic in his Las Vegas apartment. Vic's lease was up in a few weeks, and he was taking the opportunity to box more of his things up to complete his move to Nina's house.

"Are you going to miss this place, Vic?"

"To be honest, no. The best memories I'll have of it will be the times you've visited me here. I will miss Nate, though."

Nina knew that Nate was a former cop and part-owner and manager of the apartment complex. Vic had also mentioned that he was a former powerlifter who still worked out religiously—she'd met Nate a couple times, and the man was huge.

"Hey, Xana is headed back down this way, maybe she could stay here for a while? She gets tired of being on the road."

"I don't see why not, if she doesn't mind how bare bones it is with most everything gone. I could have Nate keep an eye out for her."

"The girl sleeps in the back of her 4Runner a lot of the time; I think she'll be fine."

The following day, Nina met with Las Vegas Metro investigators to come up with a game plan for Zeke's arrest. Nina had worked with the LVMPD many times during her career, and she'd always found them to be first-rate. The team ultimately decided that a simple plan would be better than a complicated one, a notion Nina agreed with. They would have Jessie call Zeke and ask him to meet her at the rock club at eleven P.M. Since the club wanded patrons for weapons as they entered, they could presumably be assured Zeke would be unarmed if he made it inside. Once he was in, undercover officers would move to the area just outside of the main entrance to take him into custody when he came back out. Jessie would not be present at the club, nor would she answer any calls from him once he agreed to meet her. Meanwhile, undercover officers would also be inside the club to monitor Zeke once he arrived.

Nina knew from bitter experience there were always unforeseen circumstances that could derail any arrest plan, but she was comfortable with it, and was glad it did not put Jessie in any danger.

Zeke hung up the phone with Jessie, a slight feeling of unease in his belly. He trusted his instincts and tried to zero in on what was making him uncomfortable. After replaying the phone conversation in his head a few times, he thought he had it: It was that Jessie had seemed slightly nervous as she'd asked him to meet her at the club, and that her usual playfulness had been missing from her voice.

Why would that be, he wondered. His first thought was that she was working with the Durango cartel or with law enforcement to take him down. He didn't want to believe that, especially when he reflected on the opportunities she'd already had to do just that. Maybe, he considered, she was in a hurry, or had to go to the bathroom, or was on her period...but he knew his mind was just inventing reasons for her behavior.

What should he do? He knew he could just no-show, but he really wanted to see her again, especially when he thought of making out with her—her with her sly tongue, the way her waist curved inward as he would run his hand down her side, and that ass he was sure he could bounce not only a quarter off of but a whole damn silver dollar. He felt his blood heating up and decided he would go, with one slight adjustment.

He never entered a building without determining a secondary escape route, and he remembered exactly what the escape route was for the rock club: It was a service entrance at the back of the building, around the corner from the main entrance. He recalled a row of plants that separated the club back parking lot from those of other businesses nearby—he would simply park in another business' parking lot, from where he could make a quick escape if he had to.

Zeke arrived in the area fifteen minutes early and scouted around until he found a parking space he approved of. It was in a parking lot for a vape shop behind the rock club, separated from it by a short wall of plants, and out of sight from the back service door. At eleven, he left his truck, stepped over the plants, and crossed into the club parking lot. He didn't see Jessie's Mercedes, but he continued to the front and made it past the security station. Once inside, he perused the club quickly but didn't see her anywhere. Leaning with his back against a wall not far from an interior door that led to the service area, he called her phone. There was no response. Zeke didn't believe in coincidences, and now, he realized, there were three: She'd been nervous on the phone, she wasn't where she said she would be, and she wasn't answering her phone. He had to exfil quickly. Pushing through the swinging service door, he headed for the back of the building. He found himself in a kitchen area in which two people were working—he grabbed his belly and said, "Gonna puke, back door." Not wanting any part of him, they showed him to the door. When he made it outside, he straightened up, walked quickly over the plants and back to his truck, then started it. No one was following him, and he pulled up to the street—the club was to the right, so he turned to the left and then made a right turn as quickly as he could. He zigzagged to another main road and headed home. On the way, he called his boss and asked for a new phone, then broke his current phone into pieces which he tossed out the window as he drove along. He had no idea what had happened, but he mentally kissed Jessie and the rock club goodbye. It was a damn shame. There wasn't anything else in Vegas he liked.

Nina and the LVMPD officers were surprised and more than a little annoyed at the way things at the rock club had worked out. They'd been watching the parking lot for Zeke's truck but then were taken aback when one of the officers reported seeing Zeke walk towards the security area—no one knew where he had come from, and his truck was not in the lot. The officers inside the club saw him for just a few seconds, but then he seemingly disappeared. It was not until they interviewed the kitchen staff an hour later that they learned how Zeke had left the building.

Nina called Sotero after making it back to Vic's apartment.

"You were right, this Zeke guy is a ghost. We had him in the building, but he got away. Please tell Jessie I'll still help her with her conviction, but she should lay low for a while. And let me know if you hear anything else about this guy."

CHAPTER 21

Abby Summers, an intel analyst who worked for Nina Vasquez in the Special Operations Division of the AZDPS, had a plan: She wanted to be a trooper within a year. During her time at college she had simply wanted to attain her current position, so she'd majored in criminal justice and was always at the top of her class. She did her share of partying without going overboard, stayed out of trouble, and worked hard.

She remembered when Captain Vasquez had interviewed her for the analyst position—she had seemed to be a truly genuine and caring person; while at the same time projecting a toughness that suggested she was not someone to mess around with. Abby didn't think she could have lied to the captain if she tried and, after she was hired and began working on her initial assignments at the office, began to see Nina Vasquez as a mentor.

After just a year and a half on the job Abby was shocked to learn that Sylvia Marshall, a senior analyst at the intelligence unit, was fired for misconduct after giving information to a cartel member. Then came another shock when it was announced Sylvia had killed herself before criminal charges could be filed against her. Abby had been trained by Sylvia and had always considered her to be very sharp and good at drawing conclusions from intel products. She couldn't fathom what might have been going on in Sylvia's head, but she used the incident to remind herself that her unit's work was serious indeed.

During her first couple of years, Abby had been happy to produce the best intel product she was capable of delivering. It seemed she had a knack for it, and she was given projects that were increasingly complicated. As time went on, however, she began to feel left out of the overall process: When she completed her work it was always handed off to a commissioned trooper, who then had the ultimate responsibility for actually doing something with the information. She wanted in on the action, and realized she would regret it forever if she didn't try to become a trooper. Captain Vasquez seemed to sense what was going on, and one day pulled her into her office and closed the door.

"Abby, I've been meaning to talk to you about your future. We all love having you here, and you do an excellent job for us. But I've gotten to know you pretty well, and you are a very capable young woman. I'd be remiss in my duties if I didn't encourage you to become a trooper; I think you'd have a long and successful career. What do you think?"

Abby, flattered and encouraged, had received just the push she needed. She joined a gym to toughen herself up and began studying for the test to become a trooper.

Zeke walked into his boss' favorite restaurant in Henderson and sat across from the man.

"Brother, you look a little out of sorts today, what's up?" asked his boss.

"Girl trouble man, girl trouble." Zeke didn't elaborate.

"I hear you, me too. I swear, if it weren't for girl trouble, we'd have no trouble. But of course, they say the same thing about us. Maybe we deserve it more, I don't know. I'm sorry to tell you though, you have more girl trouble headed your way."

"What is it?"

"I should start by reminding you that the cartel will always try to counterpunch: You hit us, we hit you back harder. It's the way of the street, where our roots are. And the leaders of our group have been very unsatisfied, trying to land a counterpunch where the little bitch Xana is concerned. You'll remember it was her and her testimony that sank a lot of the senior leadership, which caused the bounty on her to go up to five million. But despite our best efforts, we've been unable to stop her from breathing air. You've come closer than anyone, but she always survives somehow."

"Uh-oh, this sounds like we've been given a mission."

"Correct." He handed Zeke a folder. "This is Abby Summers, she's what they call an intel analyst in Vasquez' unit. The bosses want her kidnapped and stashed in one of our warehouses in Phoenix. After that, there are three things that could happen: One, she could have direct information about where we can find Xana. Two, we use her to trade for Xana. And three, we use her to trade for information about where we can find Xana. If none of those possibilities work out, then we kill the girl and leave her in a public place. Counterpunch completed."

Zeke stared at the man. "With respect, this idea of theirs is about the dumbest fucking thing I've heard in a long time. It's so easy for our bosses, all comfortable in their haciendas, to send us on these suicide missions to stroke their egos while we bleed in the streets. I think you should try to talk them out of this. Vasquez and her crew are going to come after us like rattlesnakes. And if they don't kill us all, then Xana will."

His boss held up his hands. "You are preaching to the choir, I already tried to tell them all of that. And their response was that we don't have to like it, we just have to do it. Sorry, but cartel kidnappings happen in Phoenix all the time and it's just another day in the office to them. There is one bit of good news for you, though."

"What's that?"

"If we get Xana, you still get the five million. Except for my ten percent, of course."

"Shit." Zeke rubbed his temples and thought about his mother for a minute, then began to plan. "I just want one other operator, someone with experience and discipline. Lockpicking skills would be nice. And I need to be very clear about something: If anyone tries to rape this girl, I'm going to kill him. No matter who it is."

"Understood. Let me know when you have a plan."

The following day, Zeke drove to Phoenix and checked into a hotel. Once it was dark, he drove to the warehouse he'd been directed to keep the girl in. It was a suitable location, in an industrial area near downtown and set apart from other buildings. He went inside and found a few offices in one corner of the building that would work for bedrooms, as well as a bathroom with running water. In the morning Zeke purchased inflatable camping mattresses, pillows, blankets, and enough food to last three people for a few days. He deposited everything in the warehouse, then looked around for a minute. It was depressing, everything was dull and gray, and all the offices were severely dated. It looked, he thought to himself, like a budget movie set, and he couldn't get out of there quickly enough.

He drove to the apartment complex where Abby Summers lived. Putting on a baseball cap, he left his truck and walked through the complex until he found the apartment she lived in—it was all very typical, and she had a few small plants on one of the windowsills. After making note of where he could park his truck to be close to the apartment, he left the area and returned to his hotel.

Later, he sat in the hotel bar with the operator who had arrived to assist.

"How are you at picking locks?" he asked the man.

"I'm good at it. If it's not a high-security lock, I should be able to get past it in about a minute."

"She has a standard deadbolt and doorknob lock, and she lives alone, so both will probably be locked."

"Probably. But I can get us inside in less than two minutes."

"Okay. Listen, there's going to be times when we will both be in the warehouse alone with the girl. I need to know that you won't try anything with her—you know what I mean,"

"Don't worry, I got the message about that already. But I wouldn't anyway, that's amateur bullshit."

"Then I suspect we'll get along. How about we leave here at two-thirty A.M. And don't forget a baseball hat, COVID mask, and gloves."

"See you then."

Zeke and the other operative arrived at the apartment complex just before three A.M. They parked in the area Zeke had scouted earlier and sat in the truck for fifteen minutes, looking for security patrols. There didn't seem to be any, so they quietly left the truck. When they got close to the girl's door, they pulled on their COVID masks as well as latex gloves—the most dangerous part of the mission had begun. The other operative began working on the deadbolt while Zeke faced outwards, scanning for threats. Zeke heard the deadbolt unlatch in well under a minute; the doorknob was unlocked in a similar amount of time. They drew their pistols and slid inside, silently closing the door behind them.

There were no alarms, and no sounds or movement from inside the apartment. It smelled like vanilla-scented candles. After a minute, Zeke walked toward the bedroom. The girl was sleeping on her side, facing the door—Zeke walked over, sat down on the edge of the bed, and began to talk to her calmly.

"Abby, I don't want to hurt you."

Her eyes flew open and she immediately drew in a huge breath, preparing to scream. Zeke grabbed her by the jaw as he spoke to her again, still with a calm voice.

"Don't yell or I'll have to hurt you." She didn't yell, but he could feel her deep respirations on his fingers, even through the gloves. He repeated his words a few times until her breathing slowed a little.

"We aren't going to hurt you in any way, Abby." He let go of her jaw. "I'm sorry, but we need you to come with us. I need you to get up and put on some comfortable clothes."

She started crying. "What the fuck do you want from me?"

"I'll explain when we get to where we are going. For now, I just need you to get up and get dressed." He stood up and gestured for her to do the same. She got up, still crying, but was soon dressed in jeans, shoes, T-shirt, and a hoodie. The three walked to the front door, and Zeke had the other operative walk to the truck and back, to make sure nothing was going on. When he returned, they walked out the front door and Zeke locked the doorknob lock as they pulled the door shut. When they were almost at the truck the girl tried to make a break for it. Zeke grabbed her by the top of her hoodie and shook her, hard, a couple times.

"Don't be stupid," he told her. They stuffed her into the back seat of the truck and the operative climbed in next to her. Zeke told the girl to lean over and keep her face below the level of the window, then he started the truck and drove out of the area. When they reached the warehouse, Zeke locked her in one of the offices in which he'd placed an air mattress, pillow, and blankets. He called his boss.

"Well, as far as we can tell the extraction was unnoticed. She's handling it pretty well, considering. What's next?"

"We're going to let things cook for a couple days, give Vasquez some time to realize her girl is gone. Then I'll be the one to communicate with them, see what can be worked out."

"I have a bad feeling about this, I don't think it ends well."

"You'll feel better if you get five million, I suspect. Let's just take it a step at a time, see what happens here."

"All right." Zeke was not convinced.

CHAPTER 22

Nina was slightly concerned when Abby's coworkers reported she hadn't arrived for work and was not answering her phone. When she hadn't arrived by noon, the concern escalated and she had one of her Sergeants reach out to Abby's parents, who lived out-of-state. The parents hadn't heard anything from Abby either—the news was fear-inducing for the parents and they asked for an update as soon as possible.

Nina and two of her Sergeants responded to Abby's apartment in the early afternoon. Nothing looked amiss from the outside, and they convinced the apartment manager to let them in through the locked door. Nina entered first, with her pistol out and sniffing the air for a dead body smell. There was nothing unusual in the front room of the place, but there was in the bedroom: Abby's keys, purse, wallet, and cell phone were all on a small table next to the unmade bed.

Nina called in her crime scene team to begin processing the apartment, while others from her office began canvassing the neighbors, looking for video footage of the area. Within a couple hours they had confirmation of their worst fear—one of the neighbors had a camera that had recorded a couple of masked men escorting Abby towards the parking lot. No footage of the parking area was located.

Abby, alone in a small office that had seen better days, struggled to maintain her composure. When her captors had first locked her inside, she'd backed into the corner furthest from the door and pulled a blanket up to her chin. After a couple hours, the older man—the one who'd awakened her—opened the door and set some water bottles and some energy bars inside. He'd also told her to knock whenever she had to use the bathroom.

She wasn't sure yet what her captors wanted, but knew it was a solid bet they were from a cartel: Most of the work her unit had been doing lately was cartel related. She found out her hunch was correct soon enough when the older man, still wearing his mask and baseball hat, entered the room and sat down across from her.

"You probably won't believe me," he started out, "But I didn't want this to happen. In fact, I argued against it. Nevertheless, here we are. I don't know how long you are going to be here; it's beyond my control and mostly beyond your control. There's only one way to get you out of here and back home quickly: Tell us where we can find Xana."

"Are you kidding me? First of all, I wouldn't tell you even if I did know where she is. I work for the police and you, I'm pretty sure, are with the cartel. But you've made a big mistake, because no one knows where Xana is at any given time. After all she's been through, do you think it's written down somewhere where she is? You can't be that dumb."

The man looked at her closely and seemed to decide that he believed her. "Then it looks like you are going to be here for a while; we'll just get by the best we can. No one will hurt you as long as I'm around." He left the room, leaving Abby with many questions. Had she really been kidnapped because of Xana? She hadn't been lying about no one knowing where Xana was; she doubted if Nina even knew most of the time. It was difficult for her to even guess what the cartel would do next. She looked around the dingy room, scared but trying to keep herself together.

After leaving the room, Zeke called his boss and gave him an update.

"Okay," his boss said. "That takes one possibility off the table, so we're down to trading the girl for Xana, one way or the other. You should buckle in for a long wait."

"That's what I'm afraid of, this is like being in jail."

"Nothing lasts forever; I'll let you know when I hear something."

They hung up, and Zeke looked at his surroundings. He didn't like anything about the situation, at all.

Despite their best efforts, Nina's team had not been able to locate any physical or any further video evidence that could lead to the identity of the suspects. In a meeting with her Sergeants, Nina brought up the possibility of holding a press conference to alert the public about what had taken place. There were good points to be made, both for and against the idea. In the end, the team decided to wait for two or three days: They were all leaning strongly toward the likelihood the kidnapping had been perpetrated by the cartel and that Abby had been targeted because of her involvement with the unit. Kidnappings in Phoenix were all too common, but it was the first time her office had been involved with the kidnapping of a police employee.

Two days after the kidnapping they were proven correct: Nina received a phone call from a man who claimed to represent the Manzanillo cartel. He provided enough information about Abby that Nina was convinced he was connected to the kidnapping in some manner. He was also straightforward in his demand that Xana be handed over in exchange for Abby's release. Nina told him definitively that no such exchange would be made—the man simply asked her to keep thinking about it, and said he'd call back later. Nina's team set to work to obtain information regarding the phone the man had used, but there was very little data to be had.

That night, Nina called Xana to let her know what was going on and to advise her to be even more careful than she always was.

"Set it up to trade me for her," was Xana's immediate response. "Once your girl is out of the way I'll take them out with my pistol."

"We aren't going to do that, Xana. They are probably just using the trade idea to get you close so they can kill you somehow, and then they'd kill Abby too."

"Well I'm down for it, so keep it in mind. Or maybe you could show me to them, to get them to show the girl, then your team can take them out."

"We're still in the early stages, hopefully it won't come to something like that. I'll keep you posted, and please be careful."

"I'm still just hanging out in Vic's old apartment, and I only go out for food. Luckily his Wi-Fi is still on."

"Okay. I'll talk to you again when I know more."

After a week, Zeke was developing a serious case of anxiety, and his survival instincts were pinging him relentlessly. His personality was geared towards self-initiated action, not for waiting for other people to do things in a game he hadn't wanted to play in the first place. He found himself pacing the drab warehouse floor repeatedly, trying to think of a way out of the situation. His conversations with his boss only made matters worse—during their most recent call his boss had said the cartel was considering an attempt to get Xana in the area somehow so that Zeke could take her out with a rifle. It would almost certainly be a suicide mission, Zeke thought, one which he had not signed up for. After thinking about everything hard for several hours, he hit upon an idea that could be his way out. It also carried risk and would require him to have been correct in his reasoning in Las Vegas a few weeks ago. He picked up his phone, hesitated for a moment, and then called Jessie.

Nina was about to attend a meeting when she saw that she had a call from Antonio Sotero.

"Antonio, I'm about to go into a meeting. Can I call you back?"

"If you are missing an employee, you are going to want to skip the meeting, trust me."

"Talk to me, Antonio."

"I just got off the phone with Jessie, the woman you recently helped with the old drug charge. Jessie, it turns out, just had a call from none other than this Zeke guy, who she'd been trying to set up for you. She said she had a mysterious 911 text, then a phone call from a number she didn't recognize. She answered and it was him. Anyway, he told her a story about kidnapping one of your employees, but now he wants out and is willing to provide the girl's location. Is it true that you are missing an employee? I mean, I haven't heard anything about that on the news."

Nina hesitated, but realized she didn't have a choice. "It's true Antonio but keep it between us. Believe me when I tell you I'm serious about that. How do we contact him to get the location?"

"He'll only talk to Jessie, but there's no need for any further contact; he gave her the address." He gave the address to Nina. "He said the girl is alone and unguarded for the next twenty-four hours—he's supposed to be watching her today, but he just split and she's there alone, locked in an interior office by herself. And he told Jessie he left all the exterior doors unlocked."

"Why is he doing all this?"

"He told Jessie he didn't like the idea from the beginning, and now he thinks his cartel is going to set him up for some kind of suicide mission. So he's saving his own ass, basically, but at least he didn't kill your employee."

"Well, I won't be convinced of that until I actually see our employee. But thank you for passing this information along. I'm going to call Jessie myself to confirm a couple things, but we are going to be moving very quickly. Keep your head down, Antonio."

"Will do."

Nina immediately had the AZDPS dispatch center initiate a full SWAT callout, with all members directed to suit up and report to the SWAT briefing room. Next, she had an emergency meeting with her unit in which she told them what was going on and sent them all out to establish plainclothes surveillance of the warehouse until SWAT could get there. Then, she made a quick phone call to Jessie to confirm what Sotero had told her. Once that was done, she went to the SWAT briefing room herself. When everyone was present, she gave a brief overview of what had occurred and ended with some final words.

"This is a chance for us to save one of our own. Because of everything I just mentioned, I'm authorizing an exigent circum-stances entry into the warehouse to retrieve our coworker. Once she's been extracted and the scene is secure, my unit will obtain a search warrant and go back in to process everything. Even though we are making an immediate entry, we are not compromising on safety; we'll be checking for explosives and watching out for an ambush as we move along. I'll let the SWAT Commander make the final assignments and then let's move."

Nina's team had reported no unusual activity taking place at the warehouse, and in short order the SWAT team, in several vehicles, was on the way. When they arrived, the entry team posted behind an armored vehicle at the designated entry point while members of the bomb squad, along with their detection K-9, checked the perimeter of the building. The entry door was carefully opened with a chain connected to the armored vehicle, and a small drone was sent inside. Once the drone had preliminarily cleared the interior, the entry team went inside and proceeded directly to the offices. Abby, scared but unharmed, was located and taken directly outside to Nina. Nina left one of her Sergeants in command of the scene and drove Abby to their office. Along the way Abby called her parents, and Nina could hear most of the happy but tearful conversation. Even though they didn't have the suspect in custody, Nina thought to herself, this was a pretty good ending.

From a block away, Zeke watched as the scene at the warehouse unfolded. He had to admire the tactical team members for their skill and caution, though it gave him a bit of a homesick feeling as he remembered when he had been one of the good guys. Now, he reflected, he was nothing more than a criminal who kidnapped women. He briefly tried to sell himself the idea that his actions had, at least in part, been to ensure the safety of the captive. It didn't work, and he had to admit that, as usual, he had only been covering his own backside.

He knew he had to contact his boss immediately in order, he hoped, to stay in good graces with the cartel. He made the phone call.

"What's going on, Zeke?"

Zeke did his best to sound stressed and a little out of breath. "Bad news, boss. I was just wrapping up a security check of the outside perimeter and I saw a line of SWAT rigs pulling into the parking lot. I had to run to my truck out behind the warehouse and haul ass before they spotted me. I got out by driving down the alley with no one following me, but they're going to have the girl, for sure."

"Fucking hell man, how did that happen!"

"I have no idea. The other guy and I have been doing nothing but twiddling our thumbs here, and the girl has no way to reach anyone. Maybe they're on someone's phone again, I don't know."

"The big guys are going to blow a gasket over this, and you know who they'll want to blame: You and me. Are you sure there's nothing you need to tell me about?"

"No boss, you know I didn't like this mission, but in the end I always do what I'm supposed to. That's how I've always been."

"Shit, shit, shit. Is there anything inside they can trace to you? Wallet or anything?"

"No, my personal stuff is always on me. We should both get new phones though, right away."

"Already thought of that, trash yours as soon as we hang up, I'll have a new one for you by the end of the day." He sighed. "Now I have to call this in. Wish me luck."

"Good luck."

Zeke drove slowly out of the area. He was relieved in a way, but he also knew his luck couldn't hold out forever—at some point, it would run out.

CHAPTER 23

Vic pulled into a hotel in Yakima—he'd made the drive up from Phoenix to attend the funeral of one of his former coworkers. He was worn out after the long, two-day drive, and went to bed early. The next morning, he drove away from the hotel in an inquisitive mood: He'd arrived a day early so he could check out the city, as he hadn't visited in a few years.

Meandering his way across town to the east side, he circled the block around the police station where he'd worked for so many years. The building, which had been constructed in the mid 1990's, still looked good and felt almost like home. He thought about going inside, but realized many clerks, as well as many of the officers, were likely to have been hired after he left and would have no idea who he was. He also remembered a saying about retired officers, he believed from NYPD: "When you're here you're the best; once you're gone you're a pest." Indeed, he remembered some awkward times when retired officers had stopped by—they'd sometimes wanted to talk at length about the old times, while the current officers had a lot of work they wanted to get back to.

Vic continued to tour the east side of town, which had historically been a high-crime area. He found he recognized the neighborhoods and still knew them like the back of his hand. Many locations brought back memories which flooded his mind as he drove: Here was where he'd made his first undercover drug buy; there was the scene of a double homicide; here was where a young girl had been killed, there was a parking lot where he'd gotten into a pretty vicious fight. He drifted over to First Street, a main north-south arterial, and headed north for a bit. On the left, once he made it past Yakima Avenue, was where Yakima's most notorious drug-dealing and prostitution activity had taken place long ago—now it was a parking lot and a few nice shops. Turning left on Lincoln, he left the downtown business district and headed west. The central part of town had also been the center of a lot of crime, but as he continued west the neighborhoods were a little nicer.

Taking a left turn onto 35th Avenue, Vic drove past the first house he'd purchased. Surprisingly, it looked almost exactly as he'd left it. He continued to Summitview Avenue and turned right, where he entered a stretch of small businesses that served the surrounding residential population. When he made it past 56th Avenue, he turned into a small cluster of condominiums: In one of the condos, a buxom thirty-six-year-old woman had taken Vic, then in his early twenties, under her instructive wing and had been his sweet, fun, and enthusiastic lover for a short period of time. She'd been in the process of moving to Seattle when he met her, and it was a sad day when she left. He wondered, as he sometimes did, what had become of her.

With a developing feeling of melancholy, Vic continued to prowl the west side of town. Much of it looked the same, but many things were different, even giving off a different feeling. He thought he'd have lunch at one of his old favorite little restaurants, but as he pulled in he saw that the place was now a vape shop. The old saying was true, he thought to himself. You can never really go back home.

Zeke had been feeling an unusual amount of anxiety since he made it back to his Las Vegas house. He didn't know if the cartel senior leadership had fully bought into his story of how the raid at the warehouse had taken place. His boss told him they hadn't taken the news well and were trying to decide where best to point the finger of blame. Zeke thought his many years of loyal service should count for something but also knew that rationality didn't always win out when things went badly.

After thinking about his situation for a day or two, he decided to take a couple of minor precautionary measures in case the cartel decided to move against him. He generally didn't believe in home alarms because he didn't want the police to show up at his house, regardless of the circumstances. However, for a little insurance he purchased a proximity noisemaking alarm with a battery backup and placed it on the first floor where it would detect anyone trying to go up the stairs. One of the second-floor bedrooms had a good, commanding view of the stairway and he decided to sleep there for the time being. Finally, before going to bed at night he arranged various pieces of furniture inside the main doorways to create obstacles that might give him a slight advantage if his house was raided.

A slow week went by, with Zeke only venturing out of the house a couple of times for groceries. Finally, on the seventh day, his boss told him that the cartel leadership seemed to have moved past the warehouse incident and that things felt smooth and normal. Zeke didn't put all his faith in that assessment but took it as at least a step in the right direction.

He felt comfortable enough to call his mother—he hadn't talked to her for a long time, and knew she had no way to reach him with all the phone changes he'd been making. He felt a bit of panic setting in when she didn't answer his first few calls, and he finally resorted to calling his uncle. His uncle gave him the worst news possible: His mother had died of a heart attack over a month ago and the funeral had already taken place. His uncle was in turn sympathetic and accusatory, clearly upset that other family members had to take care of the situation because Zeke could not be found. Zeke understood and apologized, even as he felt a shroud of grief settling over him. After he hung up the phone he sat in a kitchen chair, staring down at his feet, thinking of his poor mother. And of himself also, wondering how he'd come to be such an utterly selfish individual. Was there any hope for him? He didn't think so.

CHAPTER 24

Xana sat in the one chair left in Vic's Las Vegas apartment, considering her options. Las Vegas wasn't the perfect place for her to be; there were cartel members around and she'd already been spotted once, a few months ago. On the other hand, she was weary of travelling and the apartment, plain though it was, seemed to be a hiding spot that was as good as anything else she could think of. Nate, the huge ex-cop who was the owner/manager of the complex, had already told her and Vic they could use the place as long as they needed, and she felt a little better knowing the powerful man was watching out for her.

In the end, she decided to just stay where she was for another month or two, or until she had a better idea. She'd just come to that conclusion when she saw she had a call from Nina.

"Hello Nina, how are you?"

"I'm doing great, thanks, how about you? I'm just calling to check in with you."

"Well, I was just thinking about how long I should stay here, and I've decided to hang out for another month or two, as long as it's still all right with Vic."

"He'll be fine with it and he'll work it out with Nate, don't worry. Just remember that Zeke is around there somewhere, we still haven't pinned down where he's staying but he has a place there in Vegas. And the last we heard he was driving a new, dark gray Tacoma with Nevada plates, so keep that in mind."

"Will do, thank you." She paused for a moment. "Listen Nina, I'm really up in the air about where I should live long-term. I wanted to ask if you and Vic know where you'll live once you retire? I want to land in the same general vicinity."

"Vic and I were just talking about that the other day, because Doc is really pushing for us to move up to the Coeur d'Alene area eventually. It's a great part of the country, and I'd say it's at the top of our list right now. Plus, I feel like I'm finally ready to hit the retirement button at my job—but Xana, please wait just a bit longer until we decide for sure. To tell you the truth, I've been counting on having you close, wherever we go."

"I like it there too. It's cold sometimes, but maybe that's the price to live in such a beautiful place."

"Yes, and I'm an Arizona girl so it'll take me some time to get used to. Vic takes it all in stride and says it's no big deal, that it's about the same as it was in Yakima. Skiing looks fun, maybe we can try that together if it all works out."

"I'd love that! Okay, you talked me into it, I'll wait to see what happens with you and Vic."

"Perfect! But I worry about you a little Xana, all alone in the apartment for now. Are you doing all right mentally, or are the walls closing in on you?"

"Oh I'm doing fine, I'm used to being alone and it suits me." She told Nina about visiting her mother's grave and hiking up to where they'd scattered Jake's ashes. "Those two things helped me feel a little more settled, and I've been able to ditch some of the self-imposed drama I was stuck in for a while. I've come to the conclusion that, despite the past, I can be whoever I want to be."

"Well, there you go. And I'm here for you, every step of the way."

After her conversation with Nina, Xana sat for a while, thinking. She felt like she had the beginnings of a plan for the long term, and she could handle her short-term situation. However, there was a problem yet to be dealt with, and that problem was Zeke. The man was incredibly dangerous, probably the most dangerous man she'd ever encountered. His skills were extraordinary, but they weren't what frightened Xana—what truly frightened her was that the man was humble. She'd heard it in his voice and seen it in his eyes while she was in the back of the van with him. He wasn't some know-it-all mercenary who would be easy to predict; instead, Zeke knew he didn't know it all and could therefore learn, adapt, and change plans depending on the circumstances.

Xana didn't want to spend the rest of her life worrying about when Zeke would come to kill her and her friends. She lived in the same city as him, at least for a window of time. She didn't know where he lived but remembered where a couple of the cartel bosses lived in Vegas. She also knew that the cartel leadership, after all the recent law enforcement activity, would be more nervous than ever about using phones and would be holding more face-to-face meetings. It was a good time to hunt.

The next morning, Xana rented a small white SUV and stocked it with food and water. She much preferred her 4Runner, but didn't want to risk it being seen or noted by the cartel. A minivan was more suited for what she had in mind, but she remembered all too well the minivan Zeke had kidnapped her in and thought that a different type of vehicle would tend to arouse less suspicion from him. She wanted to give herself every advantage she could.

The first cartel-related house she wanted to check on was not far from Vic's apartment, so she decided to pay it some attention first. An older man had lived there, she recalled, and it had been many years since she'd seen him or been to the house. It was possible he was no longer active or perhaps had even moved out; she had no way of knowing. When she reached his street, she paid close attention to the house as she drove by but there was nothing to be seen on the exterior that provided any useful information. As was seemingly the case throughout Las Vegas, there was a small strip mall just a couple of blocks away—she found that if she parked along the edge of the mall's parking lot she could see a sliver of the front of the man's house. It was enough that she could spot anyone coming to or leaving from the place. There was no activity at the house, and after several hours she returned to her apartment for a bathroom break. By the time she got back into her rental it was getting dark. She drove past the house and noticed there were interior lights on and thought she saw a little movement inside. After driving another block, she made a U-turn, turned off her lights, and parked a couple houses down on the opposite side of the street from the house. It was a risky move, but if she could get a look at who was moving around inside she might be able to eliminate the place as a target. Using her binoculars, she studied the interior and, after a few minutes, saw a teenage girl closing the curtains. It was a strong indication that she was wasting her time at the house, and she returned to the apartment for the night.

At a little after nine the following morning, she arrived in the area of the second house. The neighborhood was different than she recalled, and several blocks—including the one her target house was on—had been cordoned off into a gated community. After driving around the perimeter, Xana determined there were two gates leading inside: A main one next to a main arterial, and a smaller one adjacent to a cramped side street. If Zeke were to show up, which gate would he prefer? It was a tough question. He'd be a little more visible while using the main one, but a little more constricted if he used the secondary one.

Without a gate code there was no way for her to get inside, but she realized the gates offered her an advantage: They funneled the traffic going in and out so that, if Zeke used the gate she was watching, she could spot his vehicle without having to set up on the house itself. Plus, she'd be much less conspicuous watching a gate rather than an individual house inside the neighborhood. She drove around the perimeter again. There were a lot of cars parked along the cramped street in the back of the community, and she could probably also park there and watch the gate. There would be some risk she'd be noticed; she'd likely be the only person sitting in a vehicle amongst the long line of cars. Things were a little better on the front side as there was a convenience store on an adjacent corner and a car wash on the opposite corner, both of which offered good views of the main gate. There was also a limited amount of street parking a little further away from the arterial which could suffice.

Xana decided to watch the main gate. She parked at the convenience store for a couple hours, moved to the car wash parking lot for a couple more hours, then took a street parking spot for a while. She returned to the convenience store and used the restroom, then repeated her sequence until about eleven o'clock at night, when she went back to the apartment. There was nothing enjoyable about what she was doing; she found it to be tedious and boring. She wondered if the house she remembered was even still associated with the cartel; it could easily have changed hands, maybe even more than once, since she'd last been there.

For the next two days she repeated her actions, with no results. She took a day off, then spent another day watching the gate, again with no results. The day after that, however, she caught a break: She was just about to go home when she saw a dark gray, new Tacoma approaching the main gate. Lifting her binoculars, she got a good view of the driver as he passed under a streetlight—it was Zeke, for sure. Zeke pulled up to the gate, paused to enter a code, then proceeded inside. Xana thought carefully for several seconds. If she stayed where she was, she would see Zeke when he left, assuming he left through the main gate. He was a wily bastard though, and her intuition told her he'd leave through the back gate. It was what she would do. The odds were he'd end up on the arterial whichever gate he used, so she tried to find a spot from where she could see enough of the arterial to cover both areas. She found one at the very front of the convenience store parking lot, right up against the arterial. It was the best she could do. She'd only been there for a half-hour when several neighborhood hoodlums, gang members from the looks of their clothing, congregated on foot in the same parking lot she was in. They noticed her right away and started calling out to her, trying to get her to talk to them. She ignored them but after a minute one of them walked up and knocked on her window—she pretended to be on her cell phone and pointed to it as she pantomimed having a conversation. The group became more aggressive and soon all of them were directly next to her window. One of them called her a bitch, and another spat on her windshield. Shit, she thought, my one chance is going to be ruined by these punks, who she knew wouldn't last a minute with the cartel. Drawing her Sig P365 from its shoulder holster, she held it under her shirt while still pretending to be on the phone. The situation continued to escalate, with one man pounding hard on her window with his fist while trying her door handle repeatedly. She had to get out of there—she slid her pistol under one leg, put the SUV in reverse, and backed away as the young men shouted profanities at her at the top of their lungs. Xana pulled forward to exit onto the arterial from the store and turned right. As she did so, she thought she saw a truck also turning right onto the arterial, but from the area of the street where the back gate was. As soon as she could, she turned right onto another street and watched her rear-view mirror closely. Sure enough, she saw Zeke's truck continuing straight past where she had turned.

After making a quick U-turn, Xana got back on the arterial, just a couple of car lengths back from Zeke. She was a little worked up from the encounter in the parking lot but forced herself to breathe slowly and to calm down. She used the SUV's windshield-washer function to clear away the nasty glob of spit, though it took three times before the windshield looked normal again. As she and Zeke continued on the arterial, she was thankful for the darkness as it made following another vehicle much easier. After a couple of miles, Zeke made a turn to the right and the cars directly behind him did not follow. Xana didn't want to turn in behind him too quickly but saw there was a parking lot on the corner of the intersection to her right—she pulled into it, raced to the street Zeke was on, and made a right turn behind him from the lot. It was only a small bit of trickery, but she planned to use every piece of subterfuge she could muster. Zeke, now two blocks in front of her, continued on the residential street for a half mile, then signaled to turn left, driving slowly as if close to home. This was the moment, Xana knew, of both the greatest risk and the greatest opportunity. If she turned behind him too quickly he may become suspicious; but if she waited too long she might miss where he parked. She drove past the street he'd turned on and sped up to get to the next intersection—there she made a U-turn, then turned right where Zeke had turned left. At first she didn't see anything, but then spotted a garage door up ahead starting to close. As she passed the garage, she could see inside the garage just well enough to confirm it was Zeke's truck that had pulled in. She took a good look at the house so she would recognize it later, then left the area.

Xana was up early the next morning to prepare for the day. She applied a little sunscreen to her face with no makeup, pulled her hair into a plain ponytail, and put on a baseball cap she used for hiking. After fueling her rental car, she drove to a hardware store and bought a small pry bar and a set of light overalls, such as a tradesperson might wear. At an office supply store, she purchased a clipboard and a padded envelope large enough to conceal the prybar. Getting into the back of the SUV, she changed into the overalls, removed the tags from the pry bar, and put it into the padded envelope. She put the envelope on top of the clipboard and left it on top of the back seat. Then, she drove to the parking lot she'd cut through the night before, angled her car so she could keep an eye on the intersection, and settled in for a wait. Her luck was much better than it had been for the past week: She'd only been there for an hour when she saw Zeke and his truck approach the arterial and turn right.

The next part of her plan required audacity rather than cunning. Her goal was to pre-break a window lock while Zeke was gone, so she could silently slip into the house later. It was in line with her philosophy of taking as few chances as possible with him. Now, she just had to do it, and she had to get in and get out quickly, before he returned.

Xana drove directly to the house and parked right in front. After grabbing the clipboard from the back seat, she walked up to the front door and rang the doorbell. She wasn't expecting anyone else to be there, but she had to make sure—Zeke had seemed like a loner to her and, she thought ruefully, it took one to know one.

In many ways, she and Zeke were cut from the same cloth. After receiving no response, she walked into a side yard, went through a gate, and approached the back of the house. There were three windows facing the yard, all of the vertical double-hung variety. The shades on all of them were closed, but she could spot a washing machine through a gap in one of them. She chose that window, withdrew the pry tool from the envelope, and went to work. It took a couple minutes and the use of all her weight on the pry bar, but she succeeded in breaking the lock while keeping the window glass intact. She tested the way the window slid open and saw that it moved easily and quietly. She closed it, replaced the pry bar in the envelope, and returned quickly to her rental SUV. In another minute she was out of the neighborhood and on her way back to the apartment.

Zeke had been in a deep depression since learning of the death of his mother. He didn't want to work out, go to the range, listen to music—he barely wanted to eat and only went outside when he had to. The cartel certainly did not care about his mother being gone, and he still had to show up for meetings with his boss now and then. But for the most part, he just sat around in his house, ruminating about how things had gone for him the past few years and reflecting on how far he'd fallen from the proud soldier he once had been. Now, despite the trappings around him, he was nothing more than a killer and errand boy for a bunch of criminals. The worst part was that he saw no way out; he felt stuck in a doom loop from which no sunshine was ever seen.

In the evening of the same day in which she'd broken the window lock, Xana prepared for her mission. She wanted to kill Zeke and she wanted to do it not only for herself, but also for Jake and for the future of herself and her friends. It was an extremely risky proposition, she knew, and it was why she'd been so cautious as she had worked through her plan. Now, she had only to enter Zeke's house, catch him asleep, and cut his throat. It sounded simple, but she knew from harsh experience there were a thousand ways her plan could go off the rails. The best she could do was to be fully prepared, alert, and ready to make split second, instinctual changes to her plan if she had to.

Xana decided to keep the ponytail and baseball hat look for her head; the baseball hat would help obscure her face if any neighbors saw her during her way in and out of the neighborhood. She also chose a zippered hoodie, T-shirt, and leggings, all dark in color in case she was splattered with blood. She'd be just another anonymous jogger making her way through the streets in Sin City, where many people worked odd hours and had to get their workouts in when they could. Under the hoodie she wore her Sig P365 in its shoulder holster, and in her waistband she'd secured a long knife that was sharp and sturdy enough to cut deep.

At two A.M., she left the apartment in the SUV and drove towards Zeke's house. It surprised her, as it always did, how many people were out and about in Vegas, even in the early morning hours of a weekday. When she was close, she parked on a residential street three blocks away, closed the driver's door quietly, and began the walk to the house. As she walked, she began to have flashbacks from a similar walk she'd made in Mexico City, not that long ago. At the end of that walk, she had killed her rapist and the act had brought her much peace of mind. This walk was different, because her target was infinitely more dangerous than her rapist had been—she had communicated with her rapist before she killed him; made sure he knew who his executioner was. With Zeke she had no such option and needed to kill him as quickly and quietly as she could. She had to content herself with the knowledge that, as long as things went her way, the last thing Zeke ever saw would be her standing over him with a bloody knife in her hand.

As she walked through the cool evening breeze, she concentrated on her breathing and stilled her emotions as much as she could. When Zeke's house came into view, she headed straight for the side gate, went through it silently, then left it slightly ajar as she entered the backyard, pulling on a pair of surgical gloves as she did so. There was no sound except for the breeze and a dog barking somewhere far away. She went to the window with the broken lock, grasped the lower section, and pushed it up, ever so slowly. When she'd raised it enough to admit her body she stuck her head inside and listened for five minutes. She didn't hear anything or even smell much, except perhaps a slight odor of alcohol. Eventually she put her hands on the sill and pulled herself into the laundry room. Inside, she pulled her weapons and held them in front of her, knife in one hand and pistol in the other. She walked slowly through the laundry room and found herself in a kitchen that had a sliding door which opened onto the opposite side yard from where she'd accessed the rear of the property. After quietly moving two chairs out of the way, she opened the sliding door part way to give herself a quick exit point, then headed towards an opening into a dining area and a flight of stairs which led to the second floor.

Xana had only taken a couple steps out of the kitchen when a bright light came on at the same instant an ear-splitting siren began to sound. She knew right away what had happened and darted out the sliding door, ran across the backyard, and hit the street leading back to her vehicle at a full run. She'd always been quick on her feet, but now her trail runners were slapping the pavement faster than she knew she could manage—she knew she couldn't best an alert and angry Zeke and just needed to get out of the area immediately. After making it back to the SUV she started it and was out of the neighborhood quickly. She cursed Zeke, his house, and the alarm. It had been a lot of effort for nothing, and now he'd be even more cautious and difficult to get to.

Zeke had been hitting the booze before going to bed, but when the alarm sounded he was up instantly, with a pistol in his hand and scanning the first floor from above. Not seeing anything, he moved to the alarm and shut it off, hoping the neighbors wouldn't call the police. He quickly cleared both floors, then secured the sliding door and began inspecting the other windows and doors for an ingress point. When he saw the broken lock on the laundry room window, he instantly knew what had happened and who had done it—it was Xana, he knew it was the sneaky little bitch as certainly as if she'd been captured on video. He found a dowel rod, cut it down to size to block the window from being opened again, and went back to bed. Before nodding back off, he shook his head a little at the nerve of her, waltzing right on in his house in the dead of night to kill him. They would, he knew, have made a hell of a team.

CHAPTER 25

Doc startled awake as his cell phone rang on the nightstand next to him, just after midnight. He saw from the caller ID that the Spokane PD SWAT commander was calling him. He picked up the phone and hustled out of the bedroom so his wife wouldn't be disturbed too much, then spoke to the commander briefly—the man asked Doc to help the SWAT team with medical support regarding a mission they were going to hold a briefing for in an hour. Doc agreed and quickly began to get dressed.

When Doc had moved to Coeur d'Alene a few years ago, he had offered his services to the local SWAT teams: With his medical and SWAT experience with the Yakima PD, his presence on missions could save lives in many circumstances. The local teams had existing paramedic-based programs of their own, but Doc's status as a physician made him a valuable asset and he was called upon from time to time.

Once dressed, he grabbed his medical bag, got into his G-wagon, and headed for the briefing. He arrived just a couple minutes before the assigned time and exchanged greetings with several of the SWAT members he knew from previous missions. The SWAT Commander then started the briefing by providing some background information about the situation.

"As most of you will remember, the entity formerly known as Preston Security is now defunct. The unlamented death of Preston's former owner, along with the arrests of many Preston drug dealers by the DEA, nailed that coffin shut pretty handily. However, our friends at the DEA have learned that four former low-level underlings from Preston have been trying to pick up where things were left off and have managed to scrape together some good-sized meth deals. They've also been quite violent and have been in three shootings so far that we know of. I'll let the DEA GS get into some specifics about that and then we'll get into the operational details."

Doc had heard the basics of what had happened with Preston weeks ago from Vic, but the new information was a surprise. He listened as the GS discussed the new dealers who, the GS believed, had all of Bryan's Mitchell's recklessness and ambition but seemed to be lacking in some of his street smarts: They had already been penetrated by an undercover DEA agent, and the agent had set them up to deliver four pounds of meth to a large distributor in Tacoma. The deal was set to occur at noon the following day. Further, the DEA had an informant who had been able, within the past three hours, to get a description and current location of the vehicle that would be used to deliver the drugs. Drug officers had the vehicle under surveillance and would, with the help of a drone, follow it once it moved.

The SWAT commander took over again and announced the plan: SWAT members would be deployed in several marked police vehicles, as well as in an armored vehicle. Once the target vehicle left for Tacoma, it would be followed westbound on I-90 until it passed the Medical Lake exit just a few miles from Spokane. When it passed the exit, troopers would shut down westbound traffic on the interstate, the marked vehicles would move into place, and a traffic stop would be conducted. The armored vehicle would move up to the area just behind the target vehicle to provide cover if needed. Specific vehicle assignments were then given, and Doc learned he'd be riding with the commander. Everyone then loaded up, and the police vehicles headed towards a staging area near the Medical Lake exit, where they could easily jump on I-90 and get behind the target at the appropriate time.

Once everyone was in position there was some dead time; the familiar "hurry up and wait" associated with SWAT and especially with drug enforcement scenarios. Everyone knew from repeated experiences that drug operations were prone to change quickly and sometimes wildly. After almost three hours, the team heard that the vehicle carrying the drugs was on the move and was headed west on the interstate.

Everyone checked their gear one last time and listened closely to the updates. The vehicle continued westbound on I-90 and in a short period of time passed the Medical Lake exit. The team's vehicles pulled behind it, moving quickly to catch up, as troopers directed other westbound traffic to come to a halt. The lead police vehicle's overhead lights came on, and the driver of the suspect vehicle pulled over onto the shoulder—however, as the armored vehicle was rumbling up next to the lead police vehicle, a man in the front passenger seat of the suspect vehicle, as well as a man in the rear passenger seat, both opened their doors and ran up a small hill just north of the highway shoulder.

A SWAT K-9 officer released his dog, who promptly caught the front passenger with a hard bite to the man's upper right leg. The bitten man fell to the ground and began screaming and thrashing around, earning himself a couple more bites from the K-9. Other officers attempted to catch the rear-seat passenger, but the man had developed a lead during the K-9 capture and they walked back to the line of cars, empty handed, about ten minutes later. The suspect vehicle's driver, who had not tried to flee, had been detained and identified by the DEA as being their main suspect. Another of his accomplices, a female who had been in the driver's rear seat, was also taken into custody without incident. A grocery bag, containing the four pounds of meth as well as some fentanyl, was located.

After patching up the bitten suspect's leg, Doc was conversing with the commander towards the back of the line of police vehicles. The commander was called up to the suspect vehicle, and Doc remained behind—just as the commander was leaving, a man charged Doc from the shoulder. Doc knew immediately it was the missing rear passenger, and figured the man was making an attempt to steal one of the police vehicles for an escape. As the man grew close, he extended his arms towards Doc's legs in a clumsy attempt at a leg takedown. Doc cupped his hands and clapped them hard over the man's ears, driving a column of air toward and through his eardrums, rupturing them. The man squealed and fell to his side, floundering around in the gravel and trying to roll away. Tracking him, Doc dropped a knee hard onto the side of the suspect's neck, which put him out temporarily. As Doc was cuffing the man up the commander, having heard a ruckus, ran up and helped with the second cuff.

"I guess that's one for the K-9 and one for Doc! He probably thought he could just get the keys from one of the cars from you, huh? If he only knew the mistake he was making!"

"It wasn't anything, really, he's unskilled. He'll need to get checked out at the hospital though, just like the other one. There's nothing else I can do for them out here."

"We'll take care of that, and thanks as always for helping us out. We won't soon forget the night Doc trashed the runner."

Doc and his wife would later agree it was the turkeys that saved them. A group of the wild birds roamed their neighborhood freely and, at night, roosted up high in the trees next to their home. They liked the turkeys for the bit of quirkiness they brought to the area but disliked the digestive messes they frequently left on the driveway and sidewalks. One morning, about three weeks after the I-90 incident, Doc and his wife were leaving their house to go out for breakfast. Doc went out to the garage before his wife and opened the overhead door so he could scan the neighborhood as he always did. As the door was going up, he saw two turkeys running and flapping onto the driveway from around the right-side corner—they didn't normally care much about the garage door and Doc headed to the right to check things out. He'd almost made it to the corner when a man, who Doc instantly recognized as being the one he had dealt with on the highway, came around the corner with a pistol in his hand. The man started to bring the gun up but Doc, while mentally cursing the judge who had let the suspect out already, brought his left forearm down hard onto the man's wrist. The pistol clattered to the ground as Doc punched the man in the throat, kicked him in the testicles, and broke his arm as he threw him to the ground. The suspect lay on the ground, holding his arm and moaning as Doc kicked the loose pistol to the other side of the garage, grabbed some duct tape from his workbench, and taped the man's wrists and ankles together.

He'd just finished when he heard a commotion behind him— he looked up to see a second man advancing on him with a knife in his outstretched hand. However, Doc's wife was right behind the man with a tire iron held high over her head, gripped in both hands. She brought the instrument down hard on top of the man's head and he collapsed next to the other suspect, out cold. Doc taped him up as well, then called 911.

As they waited for the response, Doc's wife looked down at the men on the garage floor, not liking anything at all about what she saw.

"I don't remember inviting these sons-of-bitches to join us for breakfast," she said.

CHAPTER 26

It was a big day for Nina when, after much thought and reflection, she filed her retirement papers. She still had three months to go but felt as if a burden had been removed from her back—the pros and cons of retirement had been weighed and re-weighed in her mind more times than she could count. Vic drove to a little restaurant around the corner from her office and bought her a celebratory lunch.

"How does it feel?" he asked.

"There's a lot going through my head, but mostly I'm excited for the future. I can't wait for us to get back up to Coeur d'Alene and start looking at properties!"

"Me too! We're going to have a lot of happy years there. What are you going to do with yourself for the next three months?"

"Mostly I'm going to be winding down some long-term projects and training my replacement. I think it will go by quickly.

There is one final enforcement-related thing I'd like to accomplish though, and you already know what it is: I'd like to see Zeke in jail before I leave. I don't want any of us to have to worry about him, especially so close to what he did to poor Jake. I've discussed it with Abby—she's already been doing some cellphone-related research on him, trying to pin down where he is. It's not easy though, because he seems to change phones as often as he changes clothes. But I'm going to make a real effort to get him locked up."

"Sounds good. Watch out for yourself, Nina."

"Always do."

When Zeke awoke the morning after the intrusion, he thought carefully as he had his morning coffee. There were at least two and possibly three entities after him: Law enforcement, Xana, and maybe even his own cartel. He wondered if Xana would reveal his location to the police—he didn't think so because, he knew, she wanted to kill him herself and she would never be dissuaded from that mission. He'd looked her in the eyes while she'd been in his van and it had made him uncomfortably nervous, even a little scared. His nose still hurt a little from the kick she had delivered to his face.

He knew it was impossible, but he again wished he and Xana were on the same team. His thoughts sent his mood spiraling down into depression, a feeling that had gripped him even more frequently since his mother had died. He didn't want to go to jail, but he didn't really want to continue with the cartel either. He also didn't want to die, though he was beginning to accept that as the most likely scenario to end the mess his life had become.

Zeke was still basking in his foul mood when he received a call from the cartel: He was informed of some former Preston employees who had been trying to re-establish the meth trade in Spokane. The cartel had taken a chance with them and had, contrary to their normal policy, fronted the group a few pounds of meth and a little fentanyl to get them started. It had been hoped the new group had learned the basics while under the tutelage of Bryan Mitchell, but it was becoming abundantly clear that was not the case—they made impulsive, rash decisions and had already been arrested and had lost most of the meth and all of the fentanyl to law enforcement. Because of lax enforcement policies, all had been released just a few days after their arrest. Two of them, it turned out, foolishly decided to try to kill the physician who had already made short work out of anyone the cartel had ever sent after him. They were fortunate they were still alive, though they suffered grievous injuries and were still recovering, under watch, at a Coeur d'Alene hospital. The remaining male and female, who were supposed to be the brains of the new group, were running scared and had made a vague threat to tell authorities about the cartel if they did not receive assistance in relocating. It was the final straw for the cartel, and Zeke was assigned to kill them both.

Zeke was relieved in a way and anxious in another way as he contemplated the assignment: He was relieved because it meant the cartel, at least for now, was not planning on killing him. However, he was anxious because he didn't think he could kill a female, especially after everything that had happened with Xana and Chloe. At the same time, he remembered all too well how he'd been willing to let his fellow operative kill Xana to get the reward. It was yet another example, he thought to himself, of what a ruined person he was.

Zeke realized he had no real alternative except to follow through with the mission. He didn't have enough cash to survive very long on his own, nor did he have any marketable skills outside of what he was doing with the cartel. As was the case with many cartel members, he was trapped by his greed, chained to a life he didn't want to live anymore.

Except for his internal misgivings, the mission was quite simple: The two targets, who lived together as a couple, were temporarily staying in a cartel-owned house for which Zeke would be furnished a front-door key. Later that afternoon, he visited his controller to check in and to pick up the key.

"This should be an easy ground ball for you," his controller told him once they sat down, "and a chance to re-establish yourself as the best with our bosses. I know you've been messed up after the death of your mother," he paused and made the sign of the cross. "But our business goes on no matter what, and it's time for you to get your head back in the game."

"I will…I know they sing songs about us and everything back home, but this life isn't easy. If it weren't for the cash, I think we'd all have bailed a long time ago."

"It's the nature of our work, my old friend. When we do well, we are richly rewarded. When we mess up too much or fall down on the job…" he looked at Zeke closely. "We get the bullet. And I don't want the bullet, do you?"

"Certainly not."

Back at his house, Zeke began preparing and gathering his gear for the mission. It didn't take long, as he rapidly decided on a silenced .22 pistol for the killing, with a holstered 9mm Glock as a backup. Beyond that, he had only to pick out what he was going to wear as he made entry into the house—he chose dark jeans and shoes, a dark gray turtleneck and baseball hat, and a black cloth Covid mask. He put the .22 and all the clothing items for the mission, as well as some black surgical gloves, in a small backpack. Into a larger travel bag went a single change of clothing, some toiletries, a backup battery for his phone, and an assortment of snacks and water bottles. He didn't believe in being hungry or thirsty while on the road.

Zeke went to bed early and was up long before the sun. He loaded his items into his Tacoma and was soon on the road for yet another trip to the Spokane area. The miles passed quickly, but anxiety wracked his thoughts as he continued north. He knew he could kill the male with little remorse, but the female would give him problems no matter what happened. If he killed her, he'd be consumed with guilt; and if he didn't kill her, it could be the end of him. He decided he would try to kill her, and, if he couldn't do it, he'd just have to come up with something else. What that "something else" could be, he had no idea…he'd have to think about it.

When Zeke passed the Lund area he remembered his time in the desert, fleeing from Nina Vasquez and the other law enforcement officers. The terrain in front of him looked a lot different at seventy miles an hour, but the distant hills he'd used to navigate were familiar and were locked in his memory forever. He reached the Tri-Cities area in the late afternoon and checked into a mid-range hotel for a two-night stay. After a restaurant meal, he went to bed.

He was back up at eleven P.M. and quickly changed into the jeans, shoes, and shirt he'd designated for the mission. After inspecting his hat, mask, gloves, and silenced pistol, he put them back in the small backpack, threaded his Glock and its holster onto his belt, pulled the turtleneck shirt over it, and went to his Tacoma. The drive to the Spokane house took about three hours; once there he drove around the neighborhood, scouting for an unobtrusive parking spot. There was a small apartment building about two blocks from his target, and it appeared many residents parked on the street near it. He parked in a spot that would blend in with those vehicles and shut his Tacoma off—it was a little farther from the target house than he preferred but was otherwise well suited for his purposes.

Zeke pulled on his baseball hat, put his cloth mask in his jeans pocket, and exited his truck with his backpack. He closed the door quietly and began walking towards his target. The neighborhood he found himself in wasn't the best, but neither was it the worst. He heard a man and woman arguing loudly as he passed a house that had all its interior lights on, and he made a mental note to walk on the other side of the street from it when he returned to his truck—he hoped no one would call the police on the couple in the meantime.

When he got close, he pulled on his COVID mask and gloves, lowered the brim on his baseball hat, and readied the key to the front door in his right hand. As he approached the front door he cursed the porch light—it was on and he didn't want to remove his silenced pistol from his backpack in the light. There was a screen door that made a slight whine as he pulled it open, and he saw there was a deadbolt and a doorknob lock. Sliding the key quietly into the deadbolt, he unlocked it, removed the key, and re-inserted it into the doorknob lock. After unlocking the doorknob, he gently pushed the door open with his right hand while easing the screen door shut with his left. He stepped into the house and slowly pulled the door shut, removed his backpack, retrieved his silenced pistol from it, and pulled the backpack on again. There were no lights on inside the house, nor could he hear anything, though he could detect a slight odor of marijuana…he stood still and listened for a few minutes, trying to guess where the main bedroom would be located in the single-story home.

Zeke followed a hunch and crept to the right, soon spotting the couple through a doorway as they slept together in a queen bed. He checked the remainder of the house and confirmed there was no one else inside, then returned to the bedroom and glanced at the couple as they slept: The male, lying on his back, had long hair and a beard and was snoring softly. The female was on her side, facing away from Zeke—the blanket was pulled down over her left hip, exposing her underwear. In the darkness, the skin around her hip looked unblemished, clear, and taut. He raised his pistol with its long suppressor attached to the barrel and pointed it at the center of her head—he wanted to kill her first so she wouldn't be scared as he shot the man. His finger touched the trigger, and he began to compress the pad of his finger against the metal. An image of an old girlfriend, and then of Jessie, crossed his mind and froze him. It was the moment he'd been agonizing over, and he didn't know what to do. He stood stock still for a full minute, willing his finger to pull the trigger. His right foot shifted slightly, and the small noise it made caused the man's eyes to fly open—he immediately made a wild grab for Zeke's pistol. Zeke retracted the gun to his body, adjusted his aim, and put two bullets through the man's left eye. The man went still, but the girl rolled over and looked at her boyfriend and then Zeke with wild eyes.

"Don't yell or I'm going to shoot you," he told her, holding the pistol directly in front of her face. He pulled a pillow over her boyfriend's head so she wouldn't have to see it. The female was hyperventilating but was able to keep herself from screaming; instead, she was sobbing and looking at Zeke fearfully. "Listen to me," he said. "I'm from the cartel, and I'm supposed to kill you too. You know why. Where are your phones?" She handed him one from under her pillow and pointed out another on a nightstand. He broke them both, making sure to disconnect the batteries as he did so. Then he turned to her again.

"You and your boyfriend are the dumbest people I've ever seen try to make it in the drug business. It's not for you. I'm giving you a chance—you can get out of here with one bag, right now, forget about calling the police, and go somewhere far away. Or I can just drop you right now. What's it going to be?"

"I'll leave in my car now, my parents are in S-Seattle," she sobbed.

"I don't want to know where you are going, just get moving. Don't ever come back, or you'll see me again. And when you get a different phone, use another company and someone else's name. Got it?"

She nodded and began throwing some of her clothes into a suitcase. When that was done, she put on some leggings, pulled on a pair of shoes, and left the house. Zeke heard a vehicle start up and leave. He found the two ejected shell casings, put them in his pocket, and left as well. When he passed the house with the loud couple they were still screaming, and he shook his head. Maybe it was better being single and maybe he was the lucky one, he thought to himself. Once in his car and a mile away he called his controller, even though it was still very early in the morning.

"I've met with the male, and we made a quick and easy deal with no problems. The female wasn't around, and I may have to come back to negotiate with her once she's available. I guess it will be up to our bosses."

"Okay. Come see me when you get back."

"Will do."

Zeke drove to his hotel in the Tri-Cities and got some sleep.

CHAPTER 27

The day after Zeke returned to Las Vegas, he met with his controller in the man's house. He wasn't sure what to expect, but his apprehensions rose as his boss began to speak.

"We have a problem, Zeke. Our bosses have learned that both phones belonging to the Spokane couple shut down at the same time you were killing the man, but you have told us the girl wasn't there. How can that be, you know young people don't go anywhere without their damn phones these days?"

Zeke knew the genesis of a good lie contained a heavy dose of the truth. "I have no idea. I found two phones in the bedroom with the male, and I trashed them both. Maybe the girl has a second phone, who knows?"

"Except, none of us remember you taking pains to break your target's phones before, and now you manage to break two phones, including one for a target who you say wasn't there. Now, we can't track her. It falls into the realm of coincidence, Zeke, and the cartel doesn't believe in coincidences."

"Neither do I. I can only relate to you what happened, and I can't guess about things I don't know."

"This has happened very close in time to the fiasco with Nina Vasquez' employee, another girl who got away. And when you had Xana, she ended up getting away, too. That's three strikes, my friend; the only reason you are still walking is because of your years of otherwise excellent service."

"And I stand ready to provide many more years of service, it's just a run of bad luck, is all."

"Well, the jury is still out on you. Stay close to home, and close to your phone."

"Will do."

Zeke's outlook regarding his future was bleak indeed, and his survival instincts were demanding action from him as he drove home. Once he pulled into the garage, he sat in his truck and thought hard about what additional steps he could take to stay alive if the cartel decided to come after him. He had to do something; it wasn't his nature to just sit idly around when threats against him were mounting. He came up with a plan.

First, he went to his hidden stash of money and put a few thousand in hundreds in his pockets. After a quick bite to eat, he left his cartel phone on the kitchen counter and drove to a nearby cellphone store, where he purchased a new smartphone and set himself up with a plan under a new name. After obtaining the phone, he immediately drove home to check his cartel-issued phone: He'd been told to stay with it and there was nothing that would raise suspicions more than him to not answer calls. However, he didn't want the cartel to know where he was going for the next couple of days, so he had no choice—he would try to make quick trips and to check the phone often. He hadn't received any calls or texts.

His next trip was to a nearby storage unit facility, where he rented a small unit for a year. After another trip home to check his phone, he went to a home improvement store and bought many different sized boxes, as well as several rolls of packing tape. He returned home again, thankful for his garage in which he could take his next steps in private. There were no new calls on his cartel phone. He spent several hours packing items he might need in the future—first he packed the firearms, body armor, raid gear, and ammo he wasn't going to keep readily available. Everything related to firearms went into the boxes, except for his silenced .22 pistol, his Glock 9mm, his thermal imager, and a scoped AR—those he would keep at the house for now, along with a supply of ammo for each. Next, he boxed up his camping and survival gear, as well as all the outdoor clothing he owned. When that was completed he only had a few small boxes left, so he filled them with some extra food and toiletries he had on hand. Amongst the food he concealed most of his on-hand cash, which amounted to a little under two hundred thousand dollars.

Zeke was then faced with the dilemma of how to transport the boxes to his storage unit. He guessed he could get everything in the unit with just two trips if he used his truck bed, as well as the extra seats in the cab, but would run the risk of having to explain the boxes if anyone spotted him. Alternatively, he could make several trips and just use the seats…he ended up opting to use the truck bed so he could be away from his phone for a shorter period of time. He made the first trip to the unit and back with no issues, but when he returned home after the second and final trip he saw that he'd missed two calls from his controller. He called him back immediately.

"Fucking hell man, I told you to stay close to that phone!"

"Sorry boss, I was just in the shower." He knew it sounded lame.

"Uh huh. Well, I can't remember what I was going to tell you." His boss hung up.

Zeke knew it was a bad, bad sign. He was tempted to leave his house immediately but forced himself to relax—maybe things weren't as bad as his gut was telling him they were. He ended up deciding to give things a little more time to see what played out.

When he went to bed that night, he made sure his proximity alarm was activated on the first-floor stairwell. He also retrieved his thermal imager and inspected the vehicles parked along his street—they all looked normal, and he set his alarm for two hours and went to sleep. When he awoke, he used the imager to check his street again: There was a dark sedan parked three houses down that hadn't been there before, and it was giving off a hot image from under the hood. He kept watching the sedan, and after fifteen minutes two figures emerged from it and walked slowly towards Zeke's house. Cursing under his breath, Zeke turned off the alarm with its remote, grabbed his silenced .22 pistol, climbed down the stairs, and entered a closet which, when its sliding door was opened, gave him a view of the stairwell. Until earlier that day, the closet had been filled with camping gear. He slid the door shut and waited. After just a minute he heard some muted ripping and cracking from the area of his large rear sliding door, and he guessed they had forced it open from outside the house.

Zeke figured the two would check the bedrooms first and then go back through the house for a more careful search when they didn't locate him: It was what he'd do. He cracked the closet door just enough to see a sliver of the stairwell and, after a minute or two, he saw them both silently climbing the stairs. He opened the closet door just a little more, making just enough of a gap to shoot through. After several minutes they came creeping back down the stairs, and he saw his chance when they were just a few feet away.

He took the one in the rear with a head shot, then did the same for the one in the front. He emerged from the closet, approached the men, and put two more rounds into the head of each. They were both wearing ski masks, which he pulled up to get a look at their faces: They were two of the men who had helped him abduct Xana.

Zeke found the phone of the more experienced operator and was able to unlock it using the man's face. He disabled its screen lock and went into the man's text messages, finding several between the operator and Zeke's controller. He texted the controller that the mission was complete. The controller texted back for the operator to leave the body in the house, and to meet at the restaurant the next morning at ten A.M. Zeke knew exactly which restaurant his former boss was referring to: it was the man's favorite and was only a half mile from Zeke's house. It gave him a clue as to how he should proceed.

Zeke went to the garage, started his Tacoma, drove it a couple blocks away and parked it, then walked home, keeping his garage door remote with him. Once there, he found a set of car keys on one of the dead men, walked to and entered their sedan, and pulled it into his garage after opening it with the remote. He closed the garage door, then opened the trunk of the sedan—it was nice and roomy, he observed. Going back to the dead men, he patted them down, checking for useful weapons and other valuables. He ended up with two pistols, a few thousand in cash, and a nice Rolex watch. One by one, he dragged the men out to their sedan and deposited them into the trunk, keeping their heads elevated as he did so to minimize blood leakage.

After putting on his baseball cap with the brim pulled low and making sure he had his remote as well as the keys to the sedan and his Tacoma, he got back in the sedan and started it. He drove to the restaurant his boss liked and parked it in the area his boss liked to park. Once he'd locked the sedan, he quickly walked back to where his Tacoma was parked, moved it back in the garage, and closed the door.

Zeke had not noticed, as he drove home, a small white SUV parked along the route.

There was a small amount of blood on the hardwood steps of his stairwell—he was able to mop it up with a dark towel, which he then put in his washing machine and started a long wash cycle. Zeke knew he had made some serious forensic errors, such as leaving his fingerprints and DNA on the sedan and the men, but he was much more concerned about the cartel than he was about domestic law enforcement. In any event, he told himself, he hoped to be out of Nevada soon.

The sun was coming up as he finished and took a shower, but he had enough time to sleep for an hour or two before taking his next step: He had a little surprise planned for his former boss.

CHAPTER 28

Zeke was up two hours before the scheduled meeting at the restaurant, and he began to prepare. It wasn't difficult; he'd decided to simply wear the same clothing he had worn in Spokane. Similarly, he again had his Glock 9mm on his hip and the silenced .22 in his small backpack. He also loaded the backpack with several protein bars and water bottles, and made sure his baseball hat, mask, and gloves were inside.

Thirty minutes before the meeting he left his house, backpack on, and walked to the restaurant parking lot. When he reached the sedan ten minutes later, he was pleased to see there were no blood drips underneath the trunk area—he opened the vehicle with its remote and climbed in the back seat. Immediately, he noticed a dead-body smell with which he was all too familiar: It was permeating the back seat area from the trunk and made him a little nauseous. It would be much worse in a few hours, he knew. While waiting, he snooped around in the back seat compartments, eventually finding a folded bundle of hundred-dollar bills. He guessed it was about ten thousand dollars, and he put it in his backpack.

His boss was a little late, but he eventually showed up and parked next to the passenger side of the sedan. Zeke kept his head low, knowing he would be hard to spot behind the tinted glass. When the man got out of the car, Zeke let him close the door and walk a few feet away before he made his move; he didn't want him to be able to just scurry back into his vehicle and drive off. When his boss made it past the front of his car, Zeke quickly exited the back seat and walked towards him, hand on his Glock.

"Yeah, it's me, asshole. Don't fuck around or I'll drop you right here. Walk back this way and use your remote to unlock all the doors of your car."

The man's lips tightened but he did as he was told. He was, Zeke knew, more of an accountant than a warrior. When they reached the car, a nice Lexus, Zeke opened the driver's front and rear doors and gestured for the man to get in the driver's seat. Zeke sat in the driver's side rear seat, and, once both doors had closed, patted him down for weapons—finding none, he told him to start the car and drive.

"What are you going to do with me?" asked the man.

"I haven't decided yet," Zeke replied. "It depends on how helpful you are." He knew he was going to kill the man, but didn't want to take away his hope just yet. "For now, head towards the stash house in Summerlin, and call to let them know you are on the way to pick up all the cash, so they can have it ready by the time we get there. Call them now, and if you say anything wrong I'll kill you."

Zeke knew of two Vegas-area stash houses used by the cartel to warehouse drugs and cash. They were both in low-crime neighborhoods and their caretakers were very normal-appearing people who had family in Mexico the cartel could wipe out if they stole anything. The house in Summerlin, where they were going first, was used for quick, smaller exchanges and the amount of cash there fluctuated every day. Zeke had visited it many times in the past for cartel business, both with and without his boss. The other house, on the fringes of southwest Vegas, was a main storage facility which, it was rumored, contained massive quantities of drugs and money. Zeke had never been inside the place but had helped guard shipments moving to and from it many times.

He listened as his boss spoke in Spanish to the Summerlin caretakers—his words sounded normal and legitimate. As they drove, his boss tried to bargain for himself.

"Look, what happened last night wasn't my call, in fact I argued against it but was overruled. You have to understand how things look to our bosses down south, and how they are extra cautious right now due to all the law enforcement attention we've been getting. But why don't you let me help you make a clean break; you can take this money and I'll help you leave a false trail so you won't be found."

Zeke wasn't in the mood. "Just keep driving," he said. When they reached the Summerlin house, the caretakers spotted them and opened a garage door for the Lexus. Once inside, the garage door closed and his boss was handed a shopping bag. The door opened again, and the Lexus backed out and was on the road again in under a minute. Zeke checked the bag and saw bundles of cash in all denominations. He guessed it was about a hundred thousand dollars—not as much as he had hoped for. He needed a lot more than that, even combined with what he already had to live without the cartel, and it made accessing the southwest house much more critical. He suspected there was cash in his boss's house that might also help him out.

"Let's go to your house. And on the way, you need to start thinking about how to get a few million from the other stash house."

"I'd help you with that if I could, but it takes clearance from two high-level cartel members to get money released from there. And I don't count as one of the two, so unless you want to kidnap two more of us, it's going to be impossible."

"Think harder, nothing is impossible." And yet, what the man said made sense and Zeke suspected it was probably true. As the blocks passed by, he started to analyze the problem from a tactical standpoint. Could he take the place down by himself? It would be tricky, but if he could get in he might have access to all the money. It was a tempting thought.

They reached the house his boss lived in, and the man opened the garage door with his remote, drove in, and closed the overhead door. He sat in the driver's seat, waiting for Zeke to tell him what to do. Zeke wished he had thought of bringing some handcuffs or large wire ties to secure the man's hands together.

"Do you have any duct tape here in the garage?"

His boss winced. "Yes, in the cabinet to our left." Zeke found it and taped the man's wrists together in front of him before allowing him out of the Lexus. They walked inside and sat down on opposite sides of the dining table.

"So," said Zeke. "How are we going to enrich ourselves from the other stash house?"

"I wasn't lying when I said it would take two members of a higher rank than me. I can give you the addresses of two if you want to grab them, but they both live in Phoenix."

"We'll come back to that. In the meantime, how much cash do you have in your house right now?"

"I have about fifty thousand in my gun safe, and a little more in my bedroom."

"Lead the way."

They went to a spare bedroom in which there was a very large gun safe. The man opened it and pointed to a small gym bag on a lower shelf. Zeke grabbed it and perused the remaining contents, which consisted of a variety of narcotics, some notes, and a few weapons. The weapons were inferior knockoff brands, more flash than substance— nothing he was interested in. He shut the door to the safe.

"On to the bedroom."

Zeke collected a few thousand more from a clothing drawer, and they returned to the dining table.

"How many times have you been inside the main stash house?"

"Maybe a dozen times, over the years."

"Good. Then you can diagram the interior for me, both floors."

The man told him he could find paper and a pen in a nearby credenza, and Zeke handed the items to the man. His boss made careful drawings of both floors, pointing out and labeling the function of each room as he did so. The finished drawings looked good, especially for having been done by someone with wrists taped together. He pointed out a bedroom on the main floor, which he said contained four gun safes, each about the size of the one they'd just opened.

"I don't know how they deal with the combinations. It's a couple that lives there, with no children. They are middle-aged but are always armed and they know how to shoot. Think twice if you are considering taking them on by yourself."

"I am not only considering it, but I'm going to do it, and you are going to help. Call them right now and tell them I'll be stopping by in a couple of hours to drop off the money we took from the Summerlin house earlier. Tell them I prefer to park a block away and walk in, and that they should let me in the front door so I can hand them the money in private."

"They won't like it, they usually do exchanges in the garage, like we just did in Summerlin."

"Too bad, you'll have to sell it. I need a way inside."

His boss sighed and picked up his phone. Zeke listened to the conversation and his boss had not been lying; they did not like the idea of Zeke going inside. At one point they put his boss on hold while they confirmed that money had in fact been transferred from the Summerlin house that morning. The man did a smooth job of selling it; telling the couple that Zeke had been pulled over recently by police, and didn't want to have his vehicle seen near a cartel-related residence. Finally, his boss hung up the phone and said they had agreed.

"Thank you," said Zeke, as he pulled his .22 pistol from his backpack and shot his boss twice, once in each eye. He looked down at the little pistol with admiration. He'd scarcely used it over the years, but it certainly had come in handy in his last days with the cartel.

He knew he needed to move quickly before people began missing the dead cartel members, but he gave himself five minutes to look around the house to make sure his boss hadn't "forgotten" to tell him about any valuables. He didn't find anything. Going to the garage, he placed the cash from the Summerlin house inside the gym bag from the safe, started the Lexus, and drove back toward the restaurant. The sedan with the dead bodies was still as he had left it, and he parked alongside, gathered his items from the Lexus, and walked home.

Inside, he reloaded the magazine of the .22 and began rapidly packing to leave the house for good. He knew he needed to get out of there and complete the mission at the stash house before any type of internal alarm was issued by the cartel. He wished he could skip his final mission but still only had around four hundred thousand dollars, far short of what he needed. Zeke was out of his house and driving toward the stash house in his Tacoma within an hour. In his mind, he rehearsed what he would say and do once he was allowed inside.

CHAPTER 29

When Zeke arrived at the neighborhood which contained the stash house, he drove around the area for a bit and tried to determine the best place to park his truck. Money was very heavy, he knew, so he didn't want to park too far away. But neither did he want to park too close, which would contradict the lie his boss had spun earlier on the phone. Eventually, he found a spot around a corner from the house, which was partially blocked from view by a tree in the planting strip. He parked there, put his .22 down the front of his pants where he could access it quickly, grabbed the gym bag which contained the money, and walked toward the front door.

Though his heart was thumping in his chest, he tried to keep a calm expression on his face as he walked. He was built more for outright violence than for subterfuge, but in the past had surprised himself with his abilities to bend the truth. When he reached the front door, he rang the doorbell and waited for a response with a slight smile on his face. Zeke noted there was a security door facing him, then a wooden main door to the inside—the inside door soon opened, and an intense-looking man of about forty spoke to him through the bars of the security door. After a brusque greeting, the man asked Zeke to confirm he'd brought cash to the house, and Zeke opened the gym bag to show the many bundles of cash inside. The security door was unlocked, and Zeke was admitted inside.

As he was walking through the door, he noted a fit-looking female, also about forty, holding a shotgun in her arms. She was holding it like it wasn't a stranger, and he knew he'd better act quickly. He tossed the gym bag hard at her face, while pulling up his shirt and drawing his .22. She recovered quickly, and was beginning to bring the shotgun around when he put a bullet in her upper right arm, body-checked her to the floor, and spun to face the man. The man, he saw, had a mid-sized pistol under his shirt but in the excitement was having a hard time freeing it from his clothing. Zeke put a bullet into the meaty part of both of the man's upper legs, then kicked the pistol away as the man fell to the ground. Spinning back to the female, it appeared she was trying to manipulate the shotgun but was having a hard time getting her right arm to move properly. He wrenched the shotgun from her left hand and tossed it to the side. He quickly patted them down for other weapons and, finding none, addressed them both.

"You both fought well, and with bravery, but now you need to accept that you have lost this fight. I'm not here to kill you or for the drugs, I just want the money. Now, the three of us are going to make our way to the room where the safes are: Yes, I know about them, and I know you can open them. As soon as I have the money I'll leave, and you can get medical attention." He looked at the female: She was glowering at him, unafraid and with contempt. The male was a different story—he was holding it together but clearly was in a lot of pain, and Zeke wondered if one of his bullets had struck a femur. He turned to the female. "You need to use your good arm to help him to the safe room. Let's go, now."

The man could not stand up nor even crawl, but the woman grabbed his shirt collar with her left hand and dragged him down the hall toward the safe room. Zeke saw the man was losing a lot of blood and hoped he could make it a few more minutes. He walked behind them as they slowly inched along. Twice, the man collapsed onto his face as the woman lost her grip, and she had to re-grip his collar and continue. Finally, they made it into the room, and Zeke saw there were indeed four safes lined up along the far wall. The couple moved into a sitting position and leaned back against the first wall inside the room.

"All right," he told them. "You are doing well, just a bit more and I'll leave so you can get help. Which one of you can open the safes?"

The woman just sat there, no expression on her face, but the man looked at her and, with a weak voice, told her to open them.

"Is she the one that can do it?" Zeke asked, and the man nodded. He looked directly at the woman. "Get up and open them." She shook her head, and he pointed his pistol at her. "Open them or I'm going to shoot you in the legs, then your other arm." She shook her head again.

Zeke, with the benefit of all his years with the cartel, thought he knew what was going on. He believed the female didn't think she—or her vulnerable relatives in Mexico—would survive retribution from the cartel if she opened the safes under the current circumstances. Things needed to be worse, much worse, if she were to have a chance. He decided to help her out. He raised the pistol and shot the man in the head. The man's entire body flexed, then relaxed as he leaned over to the side, clearly dead.

"Now you can open them."

She stood up and went to the first safe, the one on the far right. Her right arm gave her a lot of trouble, which was unfortunate because it looked like she was right-handed. To work the dial on the safe, she had to hold her right wrist with her left hand and manipulate the dial slowly and awkwardly. It took her several minutes but eventually she had it unlocked, and she turned the main handle and pulled the door open. It was packed with kilo after kilo of cocaine and meth, which Zeke didn't care about. He gestured towards the next safe and she began struggling with the dial. It again took a long time before she pulled the door open. The safe was empty except for a few disassembled AK-47's stacked on the middle shelves. She moved to the third. When she finally opened it, Zeke saw he'd hit the jackpot: It was almost totally full of bundles of cash, in all denominations. It was way more than he could carry, but he gestured for her to open the last safe, curious to see what it contained.

When she pulled the last door open, Zeke realized his mistake: She was to his left, and the heavy metal door swung outward to the right—when she had it open, she was blocked from his view. He rushed to get behind her, but she spun quickly and buried a knife near the center of his abdomen. He killed her with a quick shot to the side of the head, but as she dropped to the floor he stared in disbelief at the knife protruding from his belly. He didn't want it in him and grabbed it to pull it out—his abdominal muscles contracted around it oddly and it was more difficult than he was expecting. He wiggled it out and threw the three-inch blade onto the floor. Blood immediately seeped from the wound and ran down into his crotch. Feeling lightheaded, he staggered into a bathroom, pulled off his shirt, and looked around for medical supplies. There was no first aid kit, but he did find a clean washcloth, a bottle of alcohol, and a six-inch elastic bandage. Pouring the alcohol over the wound, he suffered through the burn and slapped the washcloth over it, then wrapped his abdomen with the ace bandage. He pulled his shirt back on.

Zeke was seriously debilitated, both mentally and physically, and was tempted to call 911. But his pride and years of training wouldn't let him, so he slowly walked back to the safe room. He took a quick look into the final safe and saw, to his disgust, it had contained nothing except for the knife. Shaking his head, he turned again to the safe with all the cash. He was going to leave the house a rich man, he told himself, and took a closer look. The cash was sorted onto different shelves according to denomination. The largest volume of bills was in twenties, followed by the hundreds. He looked around the room and saw several large duffle bags stacked in a corner. He chose one that had a shoulder strap and began loading bundles of hundreds into it. When he'd transferred all the hundreds, he picked up the duffle to see how much it weighed—he thought he could handle a little more, so he threw the few bundles of fifties in, then several of the twenties. He tested the weight again, and thought it was about all he could manage with his injury. It weighed, he believed, about sixty pounds, or between two and three million dollars. He would have preferred more, but it would have to do. He carried the duffle bag to the front door, placed his gym bag and .22 inside, and zipped it up. Belly aching, he walked through the house to make sure he hadn't left anything behind, then picked up the bag, maneuvered the shoulder strap up and across the side of his neck, and left through the front door.

By the time he reached the sidewalk the bag seemed very heavy and the walk, long. He forced himself to keep going, mentally counting off a left/right cadence in his head. Finally, he reached the corner and approached his truck. Setting the duffle bag on the ground, he retrieved his truck keys from his pocket, unlocked all the doors, and began to rearrange all the items he'd jammed into the back seat when leaving his house. When he thought he'd made enough room for the duffle bag to fit he heaved it inside and pushed the back door shut, sweat dripping from his face. He painfully climbed into the driver's seat, started the truck, turned on the air conditioning, and drove away.

An hour later, Zeke was still in Las Vegas, stuck in the northbound traffic on I-15. He'd left during the worst of the evening rush hour and had to negotiate the entire north/south span of town. Highway construction and a major accident had slowed him even more, but there was little he could do except grit his teeth and keep going as darkness fell. He'd known people who had survived numerous stab wounds, so he knew his injury was not a death sentence, but he figured the survivors probably had access to prompt medical attention. Zeke didn't want to get help until he was well outside of Vegas and in another state—he planned to drive north out of Las Vegas to the Idaho town of Twin Falls. There he could get to an emergency room, make up a story about how he'd been stabbed, and get treated.

The idle time allowed him to ponder his injury, and his mind began to imagine worst-case scenarios. What if the blade had punctured his bowel, and bacteria-ridden matter was currently leaking into his guts? With the thought came the realization that he was feeling a little warm; maybe, he feared, from a developing infection. And what if the blade had opened his stomach, and digestive acid was flowing out? His gut did feel like it was burning, after all. What if both his bowel and his stomach had been cut, how long of a hospital stay would that require, and where could he hide his cash and other items while he was incapacitated? Another storage unit would work, but would he be well enough to make arrangements for a unit rental and to then unload everything? He didn't want to just leave his truck in a hospital parking lot for some addict to steal everything.

His initial plan had been to arrive in Twin Falls during the early morning hours, but, as traffic started to open up north of Vegas, he changed his mind. Instead, he would get there right after nine in the morning, get a storage unit right away for his valuables, and then get to a hospital. It was a calculated risk, but one he thought he had to take to ensure his future. The more he thought about it, the more he was convinced it was what he had to do. The plan would also allow him to make a stop in Ely, which was the halfway point, to change his bandage and maybe take a quick nap.

Zeke arrived in Ely at about midnight and pulled into a large gas station that had an attached mini-mart, still open for business. While fueling his car, he noticed his black turtleneck had coagulated blood on the front that would surely draw attention when he went inside. When his tank was full, he rummaged around in the back of his Tacoma until he found an oversized button-up shirt he could put on over the turtleneck to conceal it. Then he went inside, grabbed some water and snacks, and looked around for alcohol and large bandages. They had neither, and he had to settle for a small bottle of vodka and a package of feminine pads.

The minimal exertion of going into the store left Zeke exhausted, warm, and weak. His injury felt hot and angry, and he hoped the change of bandage would help. Looking around, he couldn't find a parking spot to change the bandage without drawing attention to himself, as he wanted to take the turtleneck off and get rid of it—the damn thing was too warm and too bloody to wear. He realized he knew of a secluded place he could go, just a few miles away: The lonely road where he'd tried to kill Xana and from where he'd started his run to avoid being captured. He could change his bandage, toss his turtleneck, and then take a nap there until it was time to continue to Twin Falls.

Even in his weakened state, the incident with Xana was fresh in his mind and he drove to the location with no difficulty. There was no one else on the dirt road, and he found the exact spot he and the other operator had parked back on the fateful day. Turning on all the inside lights, Zeke pulled off his turtleneck and heaved it out of the window. Then he unwrapped the elastic bandage from his abdomen and looked at the washcloth stuck to his injury—there was not as much blood as he'd feared, but there was some and it was adhered firmly to his skin. He peeled back a corner and poured some vodka between it and his skin. Slowly, he was able to work it loose, but by the time he pulled it off he felt faint and nauseated. The wound itself looked swollen, red, and was still leaking blood. He poured a little vodka over it, pressed a pad into place, and rewound the elastic bandage. When he was finished, he felt a chill as he put on his button-up shirt and crossed his arms. The chill subsided a little, and he reclined the driver's seat—it wouldn't go back as far as he would have liked because the duffle bag with the cash was in the way. But he closed his eyes and tried to rest.

For a fitful few hours, Zeke slept but was tormented by strange dreams, fever, and chills. He dreamed of heaven and hell, sinister masked women, and angelic beauty queens. When he finally became fully awake it was dawn, much later than when he'd wanted to leave, and he knew he was in trouble. He'd never felt closer to death, and didn't think he could make it to Twin Falls. Worse, in his rearview mirror he saw a woman who often preyed upon his mind; a specter, the subject of both his dreams and his nightmares. She was walking smoothly and tactically up behind his truck, a pistol held firmly in her outstretched hands.

CHAPTER 30

After Xana's failed attempt to kill Zeke at his house, she took a few days off and assessed the situation. Her effort, though ultimately unsuccessful, had yielded some helpful information in that she now knew where he lived and what he drove. The solo, full-time surveillance of him she'd been doing was difficult and she was weary of it. However, she realized, if she could get to his truck she could transfer the tracking device she had on her 4Runner to his Tacoma and surveil him electronically from anywhere. She retrieved the device and began to surveil his neighborhood at night, hoping to catch him going to a grocery store, a bar, a gym...someplace where he'd be away from the truck for a bit. She needed but a minute to attach the magnetized device to the undercarriage of the Tacoma.

Her opportunity came on the third night, when Zeke left his house, drove past her, and parked along the street, just a short distance away. She was puzzled and had no idea what he was doing, then had to duck down in the front seat as she saw him rapidly walking back to his house. Xana didn't know how long he'd be gone, but knew she had to take advantage of the opportunity given her. Quietly, she left her SUV with the device in her hands, walked the short distance to the truck, and installed the tracker just in front of its rear bumper near the spare tire. After making it back to her vehicle, she left the area without seeing Zeke again.

Back in Vic's apartment, she confirmed the tracker was functioning and saw it had not moved from where she'd last seen it. She went to bed to catch up on her sleep. Once she had awakened, she checked the tracker and saw that the truck was parked back in Zeke's garage. Later that afternoon, however, she saw it travel to a residential neighborhood in southwest Vegas, and then north on I-15. She wondered what he was up to, especially as she saw it continue heading north all the way through town, then onto Highway 93 which led to Alamo and Ely.

After thinking for a few seconds she decided to follow him, believing she may have a chance to take him down while he was on the road. She threw a few things together to take with her in the rented SUV, realizing how nice it was to just use an app on her phone to see where the Tacoma was.

By the time she left it was fully dark, and Zeke was two or three hours ahead of her. When she reached Ely, she saw that the Tacoma was just a few miles away and not moving. She fueled her SUV, then pulled into a corner spot in a motel parking lot to study a map program so she could figure out where he was. She was stunned to realize he was in the exact spot where he and the other operator had tried to kill her. What the hell was he doing? Was he killing someone? She kept checking the tracker, but it was not moving at all. She didn't think he would kill someone and just hang around; he would want to get out of the area—the chances were he was simply taking a rest break away from civilization.

She could do the same, she thought. But she also realized the situation gave her an opportunity to kill him. As long as humans had been around, she knew, they had chosen dawn to initiate assaults—it was the time when the enemy, in theory, would still be sleeping and yet there would be a bit of light for the assaulters to navigate and to close distance. She decided to follow the way of her ancestors.

It was extremely dangerous, she knew. But the chance to catch Zeke off-guard in an area free of witnesses was compelling, and she didn't know if she would ever get a better chance. She drove to the beginning of the dirt road he was on, continued on it until she was out of sight from the highway, and turned off her lights. In the wilderness, she knew, headlights could be seen and engine noises heard from a long distance. After giving her eyes a few minutes to adjust to the darkness, she continued, just easing her SUV forward with the engine idling, and using the emergency brake to prevent brake lights from being seen. There was only about a quarter-moon, but with it and the stars she could vaguely make out the road. Several times, she had to leave the driver's seat and check out the road ahead on foot to see what it looked like.

After continuing on for a mile, she pulled to the side onto a wide spot and turned the engine off. Her map showed Zeke about another mile ahead, and he still had not moved. The beginning of dawn was about an hour away, so she checked her gear and confirmed her P365 had a round in the chamber. She hadn't planned on a night mission when she left her house, but her clothing was medium-hued and would suffice. After pulling her hair into a ponytail to keep it out of her face, she tucked her shirt inside the holster on her belt to allow easy access to her pistol. Finally, she pulled on the body armor Jake had given her. She was as ready as she was going to be.

Xana kept her eyes on the eastern horizon and left her SUV when she saw the very first streaks of gray. "Be with me, Jake," she whispered to herself as she began walking up the road. The air was cool with a slight breeze; if she paid attention she could catch the slight aroma of the desert. Her shoes were crunching more than she liked on the worn portion of the road, so she began walking in the center or the sides of it, wherever the short vegetation was thicker and didn't have branches that would snap underfoot.

After twenty minutes, she saw the Tacoma up ahead, parked just to the right of the dirt road. She paused, flexed her fingers, and drew her pistol. It was strange being back in the area where she'd almost died, but the proximity hardened her resolve. The light was still dim but it was enough that she could see her sights. When she drew near, she extended her arms to her shooting stance, watching the truck carefully. As she reached the rear bumper she saw that the driver's window was down and she continued ahead, flaring a little away from the driver's door so her pistol couldn't be grabbed. Silently, she crept forward until she could see inside. It was Zeke, but there was something wrong with him; he looked sick and half dead. He was looking directly at her as she pointed her pistol at his face.

"It would be you," he said.

"You know why I'm here."

"Yes. I... I wish we could have been together, in another time. I won't make you do what you're here to do. Take the money that's behind me." With that, he put a pistol under his chin and pulled the trigger. The report was loud, and Zeke was gone.

Xana stared for a minute, her ears ringing. She slowly holstered her pistol and looked around in the increasing light. Finally, she opened the driver's back door and found the duffle bag with the cash, too much for her to carry. She walked back to her SUV, started it, and drove up the road to the Tacoma. The duffle bag, she now saw, had a bit of blood spatter on it but she heaved it out of the Tacoma and into the back of her SUV. Then, she removed her tracker from the Tacoma and turned it off. Finally, she used some tissue to wipe down the door handle she'd touched, and pushed the back door shut with her knee.

Before driving away, she took a last look around the area. It was beautiful, with trees on the slope above it, subdued greenery in the scrub, and hills in the distance.

Xana was worn out by the time she made it back to the apartment in Las Vegas. After she'd parked, she put a light jacket over the top of the duffle bag to conceal the blood, shouldered it with its strap, and managed to carry it inside. Once she brought the rest of her things in, she opened the duffle and looked inside. It was a lot of cash, and she wasn't sure what she should do with it—maybe she could stash it in her Phoenix storage unit for the time being.

She could worry about it later. She went to sleep, thinking good thoughts about her future.

CHAPTER 31

At such events as Nina Vasquez' retirement reception, some of her coworkers often found it interesting to observe the friends and family of the honorees. Police coworkers generally knew each other well, making it easy to forget they each had entirely separate lives and different circles of people outside of work.

Before giving a little talk during the official part of the function, Nina introduced her pretty sisters. She also introduced a well-dressed couple from Coeur d'Alene and her fiancé, Vic, though many already knew him.

But there was one attendee, sitting next to Vic, who had not been introduced. She was a beautiful, composed, and fit woman in her thirties. The coworkers began to whisper to each other—could this be Xana, who'd been involved in so much of their reporting and documentation? If not her, who else could it be? There were some members of the news media present, and the coworkers pointed out to each other that the mystery guest was seated on the far outside of the room where it was unlikely she would be in camera range. They also noted she kept Vic between herself and the cameras at all times, especially as he was being introduced. Their conversational buzz died down as Nina began speaking. When she concluded, one employee, a relatively new hire, took advantage of the applause at the end of Nina's talk—he raised his phone and took several photographs of the woman seated next to Vic while everyone else was clapping.

At the conclusion of the ceremony, Nina approached Xana and gave her a hug.

"Thanks so much for coming, I know it was a bit of a risk. But it wouldn't have been the same without you."

"Some things just can't be missed, and this is one of them. I wouldn't have missed it for anything. I'm so proud of you!"

"Thank you. I can't believe I'm retired now, I still feel like I should be ready to go to work again in the morning. But I'll tell you one thing, I won't miss that department-issued cellphone! I felt so much weight leaving my back as I turned it in this morning!"

Six months later, Nina and Vic, Doc and his wife, and Xana sat around a table on Doc's second-floor deck, overlooking Lake Coeur d'Alene. Nina's house had been sold in Phoenix, and Vic had finally vacated his Vegas apartment. They, along with Xana, had been looking at various properties outside of Coeur d'Alene for some time. Vic and Nina, earlier that day, had signed the final documents to purchase a house, and Xana had made an offer on a place not far from theirs. It was a happy occasion, and they made a toast to the future, as well as to Jake, whose will had helped them out tremendously.

"I have a good feeling about all this," said Nina, "but it might take this Arizona girl some time to get used to these winters. "

"It's kind of like the tax we pay to live here," said Doc's wife. "The beautiful summers make up for it. How do you think you'll do, Xana?"

"Well, I think this Arizona girl is going to be buying some more cold-weather gear."

Everyone laughed, and they had a little more wine. Luna made an appearance out on the deck: She jumped onto Xana's lap and looked up at her, purring. Doc and his wife, who'd already had a cat and dog before the arrival of Luna, looked at each other as Xana scratched the cat behind the ears.

"She's yours," they said in unison.

The next day, Xana made another trip to where they had scattered Jake's ashes. His house in Rathdrum had been sold, she knew, and she detoured by it to take a look. A young family had moved in, and she saw them carrying groceries into the house from the shop. Jake would have approved, she knew, and the thought brought a smile to her face. She continued on to the trailhead of the Rathdrum Mountain hike, parked her 4Runner, and began the climb. It was cold, and a few snowflakes floated down as she walked. She had been reflecting lately on many different aspects of her life, and the strangeness of it all always surprised her. When she'd been in the midst of her unwanted career with the cartel she could never have imagined that her best friends, and the only people who had ever risked their lives for her, would be police officers.

She remembered when she had set Nina up to be killed. But Nina, because of her competence, honesty, and sincere effort to help, had changed Xana's life and convinced her to turn on the cartel. What followed had not been easy, but she felt like they had made it through a dangerous chapter.

She also reflected, as she walked along, about the day she woke up in Jake's front room. She didn't know what was going on at first, but remembered feeling utterly safe, as if nothing could touch her. The way she had treated their initial relationship still hurt, and she wished they had met just a little further down her road to emotional recovery. It might have made all the difference.

Eventually, Xana made it to where the ashes had been scattered and sat upon the rock there. After a minute, she started speaking. "Hi Jake. I want you to know that I'm okay. Our friends have really helped me out and we are all going to be living close to you. Nina just retired, and we are buying houses near each other. Thank you for helping to make that happen. I'll always remember you, and I'll never stop visiting you here. I love you." She started crying. "And about that man I spoke of last time I was here: He's gone, and he'll never hurt anyone again. Oh, and don't worry about Luna, I'm going to take good care of her. Goodbye for now."

As she walked down the mountain, she remembered Jake telling her about how he'd have imaginary conversations with his dead wife and son. Now, she was having similar conversations with him, except they didn't feel imaginary; they felt real. She understood him a little better.

Maybe, she thought, the day would come when, like Jake, she'd be ready for another relationship. But it was going to take her a while, she could feel it. Maybe a long while.

ACKNOWLEDGEMENTS

Many thanks to my parents and sisters, and all my family, for their continual help and support with this project! Their love and encouragement make all the difference in the world.

And to my friend Doc, who is way more dangerous in real life than I have portrayed the fictional version of him to be in this book: Thanks for your friendship over the past thirty years, I value it immensely.

Thanks as always to my former coworker, friend, and author Victor Kusske (after whom my main character is named) who really helped me out when I was just starting my writing career.

And thank you to Photography by Luba in Post Falls, Idaho, for the back cover author portrait. A great place with an awesome studio and a very relaxing setting.

ABOUT THE AUTHOR

GB Copeland retired as a captain from the Yakima, Washington police department after 31 years of police service. His assignments during his police career included working as a patrol officer, DEA task force officer, SWAT officer, and major crimes detective. In addition to writing, he enjoys hiking, woodworking, guitar, singing, and staying fit. "Change of Location" is his second novel. He lives in the Coeur d'Alene, Idaho area.

www.ingramcontent.com/pod-product-compliance
Lightning Source LLC
Chambersburg PA
CBHW022043240626
47154CB00007B/2544